THE TRAIL WE LEAVE

The Trail We Leave

♦

short stories
by
RUBÉN PALMA

translated by
Alexander Taylor

Curbstone Press

A LANNAN LITERARY SELECTION
WITH SPECIAL THANKS TO PATRICK LANNAN AND
THE LANNAN FOUNDATION BOARD OF DIRECTORS

Printed in the Canada on acid-free paper by Transcontinental

Cover design: Les Kanturek
Cover art: "The Lovers" by René Magritte © Archivo Iconografico,
S.A./CORBIS, with permission from Artists Rights Society

This book was published with the support of the
Connecticut Commission on the Arts, the Danish
Literary Centre, the Lannan Foundation, and
donations from many individuals. We are very
grateful for this support.

Connecticut Commission
on the Arts

Library of Congress Cataloging-in-Publication Data

Palma, Rubén, 1954-
  [Fra lufthavn til lufthavn. English]
  The trail we leave / by Ruben Palma ; translated by Alexander Taylor.
    p. cm.
  ISBN 1-931896-09-7 (pbk. : alk. paper)
  I. Taylor, Alexander, 1931- II. Title.
  PT8176.26.A56F7313 2004
  839.81'38—dc22   2003027088

published by
CURBSTONE PRESS   321 Jackson Street   Willimantic CT 06226
         phone: 860-423-5110   e-mail: info@curbstone.org
                    www.curbstone.org

Acknowledgments

Many thanks to Danlit for their support, and gracias, Ariel.
—Rubén Palma

Both Rubén Palma and I wish to especially thank Line and Ib
Schmidt-Madsen, not only for their insightful help in editing this
translation, but also for providing an idyllic workspace in
Humlebœk and for their warm and generous friendship. Many
thanks also to Marianne Kruckow and Lone Ravn of the Danish
Literary Centre for their hospitality, encouragement, and support.
We are also deeply grateful to the Lannan Foundation,and the CT
Commission on the Arts for support for this and other projects.
And thanks to Jane Blanshard for her keen eye in proof-reading.
—Alexander Taylor

CONTENTS

Santiago, the Summer Heat...and the Hereafter / 3

Isabel's Performance / 11

Carlos and Charlotte / 19

Just One Answer / 43

Adam and Shaha / 51

The Return of Roy Jackson / 75

Zapatito / 103

Edgardo and Teresa / 115

The Trail We Leave / 127

An Angel's Kiss / 155

Author's Biography / 169

Translator's Note / 171

THE TRAIL WE LEAVE

Santiago, the Summer Heat...
and the Hereafter

Santiago's terrible summer sun followed me all the way to my childhood's most secret place of enchantment. I had gotten onto the wrong bus and then searched half an hour for the right streets and direction. Santiago, the city of my birth, is my city no longer, even though I would like to believe that it is.

And the park was no longer called Cousiño Park, but rather O'Higgin's Park. Cousiño was the name of a filthy rich family who long ago donated the park to the public. O'Higgins was Chile's founding father, of Irish-Spanish descent, who led the War of Independence against the Spanish. Pinochet's military regime renamed the park in the beginning of the 80s, just the same as it did with rivers, mountains, whole provinces, and so much else.

Now there were paved roads, concrete buildings, a magnificent Tivoli (the largest in South America, huge billboards claimed), various gardens placed here and there, refreshment stands, a large restaurant, and—to make my disappointment unbearable—a steel fence enclosing the whole area.

The park, situated in the center of Santiago, is encircled by broad, heavily traveled, streets, but of course, more paved highways should be built with tons of cement so that the cars, too, can drive between the trees and along the lagoons. It's the same in Denmark. Every little place has to be covered with flagstones, cobblestones, concrete, or whatever, that keeps the earth and vegetation from getting air and being seen. They consider natural growth as hostile weeds and never want city trees to have more than a few square feet of soil around them. The human race must possess an innate impulse to eradicate nature.

The wilderness of my childhood had succumbed to the success of Chile's market economy. I could have spared myself the disappointment simply by staying away, but I wanted so much to experience seeing it again. And here it was.

So now I could just as well roam around a little, maybe sit on the grass under one of the surviving old trees and in this way protect myself from Santiago's sun, which has the habit of striking harder the more you try to avoid it.

As I was looking for a place where I could keep the heat at a distance, I caught sight of it—a kind of altar up against a tree. I was overcome by both surprise and recognition. For here I stood in front of an animita.

In Scandinavia, people sometimes lay flowers on a spot where a death, usually unexpected and violent, has occurred. They do that for just a few days. The Chileans build a kind of memorial that resembles a miniature church, often decorated with—among many other things—photographs of the deceased and inscribed poetic and biblical words. These memorials, which you can see everywhere in Chile, indicate the precise spot where someone met an unexpected and tragic death. They are lovingly and respectfully called *animitas* (small souls). If you see such a miniature church by a roadway, under a bridge, up against a wall, or wherever, then you say that it is *una animita* (a little soul). The place where the person died and the person's soul becomes one—and you contemplate this bespirited place with certain awe.

I was surprised because I couldn't remember any *animita* in the park at all. Otherwise, I would have claimed I knew the park as well as the back of my hand. The recognition was due to the fact that this kind of South American-Catholic phenomenon, which I tend to forget entirely in my Danish daily life, constituted a normal aspect of my Chilean past.

I approached the place slowly. It was one of the old trees, broad and strong. Around the tree there was a kind of concrete wall, not very high, but which gave the impression of framing or protecting the tree. Hundreds of pieces of inscribed wood and metal on the tree and the wall around it said: Gracias Marinita (Thanks, little Marina). All about you could see new and decades-old children's clothing and toys, nailed or glued firmly, or spread on the ground here and there.

A faded picture in the middle of the tree formed the kernel from which all the abundant scenery unfolded. From where I stood I couldn't really see what the faded picture depicted. But it was clear that the animita had been / was a child.

Most animitas live a quiet and anonymous life. They are cared for by family and friends, who now and then come to light candles and set out fresh flowers. Others, very old animitas, fall into decay and become what we all will be one day: earth and dust.

But there are some which in time become known for being *milagrosas* (miraculous) in the sense that it is claimed that they can perform miracles. These miracles are in most cases assistance related to personal problems or crises: debt, unemployment, divorce, love, housing, sickness, family conflicts, and so on. When I was a child, there was always someone who approached an animita to get help from the beyond. And I never thought about it. That's just the way it was.

The animita I stood in front of was undoubtedly very milagrosa. The ornamentation around and on the tree was overwhelming, with hundreds of expressions of gratitude.

There were some people in the midst of praying, probably the usual Our Father and Ave Maria. Others lit candles in order "to pay" for one or more favors the animita had done for them. Some children sat silent and still on a bench, gazing at the tree and its altar-like additions.

After a few minutes, where I, too, felt a strange awe of the tree's all too clear suggestion of another life next to or beyond this one, I went over to an older man, of some sixty something years, who from his modest stall sold small items: candles, matches, and cigarettes. I asked, "What happened to the little girl?"

He looked at me calmly for a long while, and answered, "It was 1945. She was raped and murdered, her throat cut by her stepfather. Right there, by the tree. She was five years old."

"It's strange," I said, "but when I was a child, I came here and played. I've swum in the lagoon, climbed the trees right around here... And I don't remember at all seeing the animita."

He smiled knowingly. "Of course you saw it—but yet without seeing it anyway. There are things you only notice when you get older."

In order to encourage him to continue, I didn't answer.

He said, "Look, my mother took care of the animita her whole adult life. And only when she died did I find out what she had done. Since then I've come here every single day, nearly 16 years now, and have continued my mother's work."

I sat down on a big stone on the other side of his stall. He had grown up in the same poor neighborhood as I had. And what a coincidence! We had both, each at his own age, witnessed a dramatic escape from the nearby prison for hardboiled criminals.

Suddenly we became a little serious. And we talked about the lot of the poor, about a man's duties, about fate, about life after death, and naturally also about God, who certainly had had some purpose in sending us wandering about in this world.

We grew silent a few minutes. A woman knelt in front of the tree, prayed, laid some flowers here and there, and lit some candles. Then she made the sign of the cross as if she were on her way out of church and left.

As far as I know, the Catholic Church has always avoided taking a stand on the subject of *animitas milagrosas*. Strictly speaking, the phenomenon is not Christian at all. But the

Catholic Church learned a long time ago that it was pretty hard to maintain theological principles in South America.

I said, "From your stall here, you must have seen many things."

"That I certainly have," he said as if he were speaking to himself.

I asked him to tell me something extraordinary he had witnessed. But he didn't want to, and gave me some reasons. But I insisted until he relented. He gazed for a moment toward the lagoon while he searched for a story to tell me. Then he looked again at the tree, "I can tell you the story of the flagstones."

I had noticed that flagstones covered a number of square meters in front of the tree.

"It happened years ago, before the military renamed the park and fenced it in. It was a Monday, very late in the evening. You know, Monday is the animitas' day."

I nodded, affirmatively, even though I didn't know it.

"I sat here where you see me now and smoked a cigarette. An old man was bringing a gift to the animita. He prayed, I guess. There were only us two, each in his own corner of the night. It was very quiet."

"Another man came from over there (he pointed), walking over from those bushes. The man was around forty, well dressed. He asked me whether the animita could help him. He was really very upset. I replied what I have replied to lots of desperate people who have come here. I said very simply that if he didn't have anywhere else to go for help, he might just as well try here...with the animita.

"The man told me that he had lost his motorcycle, an expensive German BMW. He worked at a place outside of Santiago, well off the beaten track. His whole family depended on the motorcycle. Without it, he would simply lose his job.

"You know, it was in those misery times, the first years under the dictatorship, when most Chileans were literally starving. The man didn't have the slightest chance of buying a new motorcycle. He looked as if he were ashamed when he asked again if I thought the animita could help him find his motorcycle.

"But then something happened. The old man who had now finished his business in front of the tree, came over unexpectedly and said, 'Excuse me. But it's a very quiet night, and while I was praying in thanks to the animita, I couldn't help overhearing your conversation. I found a motorcycle.'"

"Well, it turns out a motorcycle had been left for a number of days in front of the old man's home. It had obviously been stolen and dropped there. He didn't want to go to the police because he didn't want to get mixed up in things that could make his life more difficult than it already was. Everyone was afraid of the police under the dictatorship. He had taken the motorcycle in, and now it lay in his back yard, covered with an old rug.

"Asked about the make of the motorcycle, the old man answered he had no idea at all about that kind of thing. But it was simply a matter of going to his house to see. I watched them go off together.

"Almost an hour later the man was back, more excited than before. It was his expensive, German motorcycle in the old man's yard! I have to honestly admit that in spite of all the unbelievable things I have seen over many years, I had difficulty believing my own eyes.

"The man was dumbfounded. This was the miracle that would save his family's future. On the other hand, it had all seemed so simple and fortuitous that it was absurd to call it a miracle. He hadn't even managed to ask the animita for anything whatsoever. Still dumbfounded, the man looked at me. Was it the animita that had helped him from the beyond...or what?

"I answered that it was up to him to decide.

"The man considered the question. In spite of everything, it was here by the tree that his anguish had found an end.

What if it really was the animita that had gotten his motorcycle back? In that case, he couldn't allow himself to just leave as if nothing had happened. He looked at me…and I just looked back at him. It was his decision.

"'What can I do for the animita?' he asked me.

"I told him the winter rain turned the area around the tree into a real mud puddle, and people got their clothes and shoes muddy. What about some flagstones?

"The day after, at noon, two workers came, and when they left, the area in front of the tree was paved with flagstones."

I couldn't help thinking what the courts of Copenhagen's District would say if someone, for example in H. C. Ørsted's Park, began to lay flagstones in front of a tree. Yes, all in all, what would the Danes say if a public tree was decorated in every possible way, and then worshipped as a miraculous shrine?

"That was the story of the flagstones," he concluded in his nearly too straightforward manner. He added, "But I can easily tell you that every single inscription of gratitude, every single thing that decorates the tree, has a story."

He pointed to a sign that was written in poor Spanish, filled with spelling errors.

"On a Greek ship an Arab sailor told a Chilean sailor about his incurably ill daughter. The Arab and the Chilean came here and asked the animita, who was also a little girl, to cure the Arab's girl. They kneeled together before the tree. Months later the Arab came alone. He nailed a sign firmly on the tree, bought 40 candles from me, lit them all at the foot of the tree, and left. He looked happy."

I asked, "Have you yourself ever asked the animita for anything?"

"Never." He glanced at the sky. "As God is my witness. But if I get in a fix someday, I wouldn't hesitate to ask the animita for help. That's the way it is."

After a long silence, he said, "There is something about the way you speak. Have you lived abroad, perhaps?"

Suddenly I felt myself caught in a lie. And I had to remind myself that I had at no point lied. I had simply not told him I didn't live in Chile. The omission had certainly been a kind of lie. I had only wanted to seem as Chilean as possible in order to win his trust and make him speak about the animita. Half a life in another country gives rise to certain schizophrenic traits.

"I live in Denmark," I said then, and I could hear that it sounded like an unwilling confession.

"Denmark," he said thoughtfully, as if he knew something about it. "And can you make do in Denmark?"

"Yes, I believe I can."

"I'm glad to hear someone from my neighborhood is doing well, far away in another country."

I thanked him, got up, and reached out my hand to say goodbye.

He held my hand a moment. "I want to wish you a good life in Denmark. And may the Almighty always protect you."

Some minutes later, as I went in the direction of the nearest subway, it struck me that Chileans fairly often speak about the soul, the hereafter, God, and the like.

But maybe it was only in comparison with the Danes that I thought so. Maybe the Chileans spoke just so much about such things as they should, no more, no less.

I stopped at a water faucet and splashed a lot of water over my face.

Had it always been so warm in Santiago?

Isabel's Performance

At last…at last Isabel appears on the stage. The bright stage lights force her to blink. And all these eyes observing her are like a wall she has to push away in order to move forward. Her mother and Lars are sitting out there somewhere in the dim and jam-packed gymnasium, holding hands as usual. With quick, short steps, Isabel finds her place and lies down on the sofa.

Her heart…her heart starts beating in her chest, throat and ears. Suddenly she is not only nervous but afraid, too. Why? She certainly remembers her lines in Danish all right.

In school in Playa Verde you always had to memorize. At any moment, Señor Barros could ask you about the capitals of different countries, the world's largest rivers, and the names of the Spanish conquistadors and the founding fathers of Chile. And Isabel was quick to give the right answers. If only she were back in Playa Verde and Señor Barros was asking the class: What's the name of the author who wrote "The Swineherd"? Then she would promptly and confidently answer: Hans Christian Andersen!

But Isabel is in Vestervig's school now, in the middle of a school play, and is waiting for Mette, the princess who has kissed the swineherd, to come tumbling in and exclaim, "Oh, nej!" And immediately Isabel, the Lady-in-Waiting, will "wake" and say what she has to say…in Danish and without hesitation: "Hvad sker der, min princess? De ser jo so oprørt ud!" Which she knows should be pronounced: "Va squea ra, min pgrinses? Di sea llo so obgreort ud!" Then Mette will repeat: "Oh, nej!" And the next line, which Isabel has tucked in her memory, is: "Fortæl, fortæl Princess, hvad sker der?" And this should be pronounced: "Fotchel, fotchel, pgrinses. Va skea ra?"

Countless times she has read the Danish text, and as many times she has, both aloud and to herself, recited it the way it should be recited. Strange people, the Danes, they don't talk the same way they write.

But what is it that makes her so afraid?

Isabel clenches her fists to give herself courage. But instead it seems as if the fear spreads along her back and legs. And her heartbeat—it is unbearable. Beautiful Diosito, help me, she says to herself. You can always ask God for help if you're afraid—that's what Father Facundo and Sister Antonieta said to the children of Playa Verde.

Her mother and Lars—she must make them proud of her! Only two months in a Danish school and already she is in a play. Since she came to Vestervig's school, she has tried her best to do everything as well as possible. It has to go well; it just has to.

Once again Isabel recreates the sound of the first answer in her inner ear: "Va squea ra, min pgrinses? Di sea llo so obgreort ud!" And then the next, which comes right after Mette's second line; "Oh, nej!" and which sounds like: "Fotchel, fotchel, pgrinses. Va skea ra?"

Yes, here in Vestervig, Isabel wants to be just as good at remembering things as she was in school in Playa Verde.

Playa Verde—so far from the nearest city. It took two hours for the old, crammed bus, moving slowly and coughing like Father Facundo, to come out of the mountains, and then you could see the whole port city of Valparaiso, far below, pasted to the sea, spread across the coast and the hills like a huge spider web of streets and buildings. And late in the afternoon, the bus got ready to return to Playa Verde. People were already streaming into the bus stop on the Plaza Independencia—whole families with shopping bags and boxes, older school children, and those working in offices, in the harbor, or selling goods in the streets, and, of course…the eternal drunk who sold those birds that were just as noisy in their cages as he himself on the bus. And once again the old bus pulled itself out of the port city and found its pot-holed and dusty road, first up the hills, then up the mountains and into the forest, where farm workers and laborers with their shovels, rakes, and wheelbarrows were gathered up. And you rode helter-skelter together while the drunken man sang and the birds made a racket and people asked him to shut up because he was intolerable. And right after the police station the sea appeared, the deep endless blue to the right of the bus, and soon you would be back in Playa Verde, where everyone knows each other and what is going on that evening, the next day, and all the coming days, and you talk with one another in the same way that you write…and you speak Spanish with everyone, not only with your mother, like here in Vestervig where no one but her mother speaks Spanish and all the rest speak Danish.

From Playa Verde to Vestervig. It seems to Isabel that one day she was in Playa Verde on her way to the supermarket in Valparaiso and the next day they lived in Vestervig with Lars. It was because of the cardboard box, the cardboard box jammed with goods and so heavy that they could barely carry it out of the supermarket. And there she walked with her mother—the many streets down to the bus stop on Plaza Independencia, while the cardboard box weighed them both down and threatened to burst. Suddenly the big gringo showed up—blond hair, eyes as blue as if they were made of glass. He talked funny and he lifted the box without any effort, and they continued, all three, down the street. At the Plaza Independencia the gringo and Isabel's mother talked together while people all around them bellyached because the bus was late again. Isabel drew hopscotch squares on the ground, took her hopscotch stone—an empty can of shoe polish—out of her pocket and began hopscotching. Once in a while she lifted her eyes from the lines on the ground—and saw her mother smile as she had not smiled in a long, long time. Her mother and the gringo, who was called Lars, continued to see each other; later they wrote to each other, and then came that strange day when her mother held Isabel by the hand and prayed to God and San Cristobal, the protector of travelers, because they were to set out on a long journey to Denmark—to Lars in Vestervig.

Time passes so slowly when you have to wait. Your body gets stiff and your fear grows. Isabel figures that Majken, the other Lady-in-Waiting, must already be on stage, not too far from her and already combing her hair in front of the big mirror on the back wall of the stage. But Isabel cannot hear anything. Is she still alone on stage? The whole play will be ruined if she turns her head and opens her eyes to look around. And yet, what if she tried…just a little bit? Isabel doesn't know whether it's because she is afraid or because she isn't able to, that she can't move her body the least bit.

Oh, Diosito…in Playa Verde she was always confident when she stood in front of the teacher and the other students, or in front of the whole school, for that matter. Isabel repeats the necessary sentences again: "Va skea ra, min pgrinses? Di ea so…so…" But it is as if her memory drains away to nothing. God! How is it the first line continues? Was it…Di sea yo sodan…? Or…Di er so…so… These Danish sounds seem to flow into each other—until a shiver runs through her body and makes it cold. Because she has forgotten how the sentence continues!

She skips to the next sentence, the one that began with "Fotchel, fotchel"…and meets again the terrifying emptiness within her head. She strains to remember, but without success. Her memory seems locked tight—it can no longer find the right sounds.

If only she were alone and far away, like in the days after her father left when she drew hopscotch squares in the sand on the little beach in Playa Verde. She drew the lines with a branch the waves had washed ashore, but she did not hopscotch. Every once in a while she stopped and looked toward the tiny houses of Playa Verde at the foot of the green mountains—and there is the tiny wooden house where her mother cries and to which her father will never return. Only the sea and the wind keep her company, and she stares once more at her hopscotch squares but she doesn't hopscotch... some tears fall and become dark little dots as soon as they hit the sand, but then the wind comes, as tireless as the sea, and the dark dots disappear and suddenly it's as if the tears never fell. If only Isabel could cry now, here in Vestervig...but she knows she must not do that.

Her mother and Lars are sitting out there waiting anxiously for her to get up and perform. The packed gymnasium, the teachers, and the girls and boys in the play are waiting, too. A whole world is waiting for Isabel, who is lying motionless, gripped by an anxiety greater than herself. The sounds she was able to remember until a moment ago are gone...and will not come back. Oh beautiful Diosito! What has gone wrong?

In Playa Verde nothing would have gone wrong. In Playa Verde she would never have disappointed her mother; she never would have disappointed anyone. But Playa Verde is farther away than ever. Playa Verde—the tiny houses between the green mountains and the sea that hums day and night and the most at night. And the creaking wooden church, the altar with the crucified Jesus, who has to suffer so mankind can find the way to Heaven. And old white-haired Father Facundo, who takes care of the church's garden while he talks to sleepy Yaco, the stray dog that is in reality his, or perhaps the church's...who knows? On Sundays, Sisters Antonieta and Pilar come from Valparaiso, both young and good-humored; they teach the catechism...about the Trinity and the Resurrection and the Sacraments and a whole lot of other things children don't really understand at all. On the other hand, they all understand the difference between Heaven and Hell. Into heaven come all the souls of good people after death...and everything is beautiful, and the angels of God look after them. Hell is just the opposite...the evil ones burn in flames while they are tortured by the Devil and his little devils. In one place you have a beautiful time; in the other a horrible one. But both Father Facundo and Sister Antonieta have said children always go to Heaven, because the things they do wrong they don't do on purpose.

And it is not on purpose that Isabel has forgotten what she has to say—Diosito lindo, not on purpose. She wants with all her heart to make her mother and Lars happy and proud of her. Her heart; it's beating so hard, it seems it will explode any moment. What is happening around her? She would like to be far away from everyone and everything, but she has to be on the sofa and wait…Wait for what? Oh, God!

With great clarity, Isabel remembers the time she asked Sister Pilar whether it was possible to see the soul. It is in the backyard of the church, and the Sister is sitting on a wooden chair facing the children, who are sitting on the ground while she explains that once in a while it is possible to see the soul—like a floating puff of breath that comes out of the mouths of children who have just died. Children are not sinners, and so this little soul-puff flies right up to Heaven, where the Lord and all the angels welcome it.

Unexpectedly, Isabel feels a blow inside her chest—like a pain moving up out of her throat and making her mouth open slightly. The pain shoots upward more quickly and hits the darkness behind her closed eyes. And in a short, nearly imperceptible moment, a light explodes inside Isabel's head. Immediately after, she is weightless and floating both inside her body and out in space simultaneously. Strange, she is not afraid. On the contrary, everything seems so quiet and peaceful. Then she detaches herself slowly from her body until she can no longer sense the sofa on which she is lying. And there is nothing to be afraid of. Things are just as they should be.

Now Isabel hears the shouts of children and adults right around her—"Isabel! Isabel!" And she sees a crowd of adults with their children, who are running around in circles on the Plaza Verde square when she is a little girl, three years old, holding her mother's hand. And Isabel feels the reassuring joy at holding her mother's hand and waving to the children running around in the square. Isabel is both inside and outside herself as a little girl—now a little girl at her fourth birthday party, and there are grownups and noisy children around the table. Her father and mother stand in the doorway smiling joyfully because Isabel is blowing out the candles on her birthday cake. The children shout: "Isabel!" Her mother shouts: "Isabel, darling. What's happening?"

The light in the candle flames grows and grows—that's what's happening, Isabel thinks fleetingly. And the light rises and grows big—big as the sun, like a shining ball deep in the heavens…in the heavens where the angels of the Lord sing so beautifully when they bid the good souls welcome. The song fills the space and forgives every wrong thing you have done without thinking about it. "How beautiful…Diosito lindo, how beautiful it is." Isabel's inner voice comes out of her heart and becomes one with the angels' song, which forgives and welcomes.

Isabel feels herself being shaken, being slapped in the face. And she sees herself from above while she is still lying on the sofa in her Lady-in-Waiting dress. Lars is standing on the stage, too. Right next to him is Mette, dressed like a princess, and Majken, as a Lady-in-Waiting. "Isabel! Isabel!" they say while they are crying. Her mother and the drama teacher are kneeling over her. Her mother shakes her, slapping her face. Sobbing, she cries: "My darling! My darling come back!" Suddenly Isabel is back in her own body and in a flash looks up at her mother's tearful face. Isabel can't understand her mother's concern. Why is she crying? And then again she is up above, looking down at herself lying motionless on the stage, surrounded by desperate people. The song of the angels reaches her again. And she turns away from the stage. The heavens spin round in huge whirls, opening a path in the center, right in front of her—and at the end of that heavenly path is the radiant ball, God in all his splendor. And Isabel is happy, happier than she has ever been.

"Isabel, darling—don't leave me!" Her mother is crying and keeps on shaking her and pinching her cheeks.

Isabel hesitates, she finds herself between Heaven and a life in Heaven and her mother and life in Vestervig. She loves her mother, and that is the only reason she would return to a life in Vestervig.

And it is right now, Isabel knows—it is right now she has to choose.

Carlos and Charlotte

It is an exaggeration to say that love makes you blind. I think it's more that love weakens intellect and blurs reality. That's why lovers are so easily mistaken about each other. For the same reason, real love stories are always complicated, having at times an incomprehensible dramatic element.

Carlos came into the world in a gray and dusty city, a real dump situated in the middle of the Atacama Desert, said to be the harshest, most barren desert in the entire world. Early in his twenties and hungry for experience, he set his feet down in green and fertile Denmark. When he reached thirty, and after a lot of salsa dancing and a number of different, temporary Danish girlfriends, he settled down with the slightly younger Mette in a Copenhagen suburb. He was really in love with Mette, whom he thought both beautiful and intelligent. Being with her, he felt that the so-called cultural differences were at best nothing more than a tiresome topic for discussion.

Carlos looked to the future. Certainly he had had his fill of Copenhagen's capricious nightlife. It was time to settle down, begin a new life out in the suburbs—with Mette.

With that in mind, Carlos registered for a Danish course in evening school. The years in Denmark had made him a better salsa dancer than he had ever been in Chile, but on the other hand, his everyday Danish was halting. An eventual future education would undoubtedly demand better linguistic proficiency.

And while Carlos tried twice a week to become more knowledgeable about the many rules, and the just as many exceptions, for the Danish language, he did not notice that his blonde teacher, Charlotte, observed him with increasing interest.

For Charlotte the lessons had acquired an entirely new content. There was something about the ten-year younger Chilean. His dark eyes, his accent, the mild but inviting smile—everything about him attracted her. When she was with Carlos (the very few times they exchanged a few words during the breaks), she felt herself in possession of a womanliness she had never experienced with her husband, Peter.

As often before, the language teacher once again was aware of the insufficiency of language when it came to matters of feelings and moods. It was as if suddenly there were more woman inside her, and she lacked the words to name these different experiences of her own sex.

Charlotte's relationship to Peter rested on many years of marriage, two children, deeply rooted sexual habits, and a common social life. A secure life, not the least of which, economically. Her work as a teacher had no other purpose than not being bored at home. In the light of the income that Peter's companies provided, her teacher's salary seemed a joke.

Right in the middle of this stability, the fantasies about Carlos grew from the naïve to the alarming. She began, literally, to dream about him within a broad spectrum that went from a chance meeting downtown, which led to an innocent conversation at a café…until he, like a wild animal, screwed her with her clothes on right in the classroom. Naturally, before Carlos showed up, she had from time to time fantasized about sexual experiences with exciting strangers. But this had not awakened the slightest moral concern. Because sexual fantasies belonged to the world of fantasy; that is how she always looked at it. But suddenly to fantasize about a man she came into contact with on a regular basis…well, that was alarmingly different.

But why think these kinds of thoughts at all? She certainly had a good life with Peter and their two wonderful children. And Peter loved her with a devoted and unconditional love. What man, after 20 years of marriage, kept on saying things like, "You are beautiful...I love you."? His love obligated her.

Charlotte took up the battle—an intense battle against these troubling thoughts about Carlos. And, predictably enough, the more she fought them, the more gnawing they became.

The situation worsened for good the evening she ascertained that Carlos showed more than a student's interest in her. It happened during the class break. Carlos had said, "Excuse me, can I get by?" and laid both hands on her shoulders in order to move her out of the way in a friendly fashion. He had unquestionably held her longer than necessary. And then, before his hands left her shoulders, she noticed a gentle but definite squeeze.

That night Charlotte could not fall asleep. Carlos's hands still touched her shoulders. But it was only Peter who lay beside her, sleeping his usual innocent sleep. Suddenly everything became quite clear. She would sleep with Carlos if the opportunity turned up. And only then would she consider whether what she had done was right or wrong. What had happened forced her to be consistent with herself first and foremost. She gazed intently into the room's darkness. What would happen the next time she and Carlos met?

They met the next day and...yes, she was completely shattered. Carlos sent her subtle, nearly imperceptible signals that he yearned for her just the same way she yearned for him. But when the lessons were over, she had to go home.

Why did she have to go home to her husband every day when her whole body longed to be with Carlos? Life was hard. Life was illogical.

About a month later, life showed itself infinitely more gruesome. The course for foreigners came to an end. And

Carlos was gone. The subtle signals they had exchanged, all the closeness they had built up—everything was lost. For Carlos was married. Just as she was.

Charlotte wandered through shadows. And she was beside herself that day she went into the main railway station, bought four postcards for 10 kroner, and sat down at a café table. Two merciless months had passed since the final day of the course, and the abyss between her and Carlos grew steadily. Would he be able to remember at all when he had laid his hands on her shoulders? What about the time they stood in the doorway and couldn't decide who should go out first...? And then that time he couldn't find his ballpoint...and she pointed out to him that it was under his notebook? Little things that meant so much. The first three postcards were torn into pieces before she decided on the following: "I hope you are well. I want you to know I think of you day and night. These months without seeing you have been the worst of my life." The signature read: "One who can't forget you." The card was sent from the post office in the main station.

Out on the street, she breathed easier. Before she had gone into the railway station, Carlos had been far away. Now he had moved closer. Tomorrow he would read the card— and he would know at once who was behind the message.

The next day Carlos sat at the breakfast table across from Mette and looked at the postcard. He read the card with the greatest attention, many times. He ascertained where it was sent from and which post office. He scrutinized the round, well-formed script, which undoubtedly belonged to a woman. He studied the image: the Little Mermaid, a stature he had not seen for many years. He went through all the imaginable and unimaginable women who might have sent it. And then he gave up. He had not the faintest idea who could send him the card like that. He looked at Mette, his face a question mark.

But Mette had no doubts. The card was screaming proof that Carlos, at least within the past few months, had been involved with another woman. He maintained his innocence the best he could. But what could he do against such overwhelming proof?

At first Mette was hurt and furious. Then came some ominous days when she didn't say a word, but now and then threw him the strangest glances. Finally she spoke. For his information…that time she went on a charter tour with her friend Tina to Greece, she had slept with a Greek—it lasted the whole final week of the trip. Well, then, if she had to accept his peccadilloes, he had to accept hers, too.

And now it was Carlos's turn to be hurt and furious. Mette's infidelity completely overshadowed the mystery of the postcard's sender. He called her a miserable bitch who found pleasure in screwing Greeks. And God only knew what other strange nationalities she was also accustomed to enjoying in bed. Her immediate answer was that his cheating had just been exposed—typical Latin American macho who did not have the slightest idea about modern Danish values of equality. Naturally there followed a cascade of mutual accusations and mud-slinging. The storm lasted about two exhausting weeks—until they split up.

In the meantime, Charlotte came to terms with herself and to the fact that Carlos wasn't going to respond to the postcard. He had a marriage and a life to get on with. And so it was a real shock when during a busy sale day she ran into him in the cafeteria of Magasin du Nord. After a few awkward initial words, they sat down to talk. With nervous politeness Charlotte asked how he was.

Carlos answered that a lot had happened since they last saw each other—among other things, he was alone.

Charlotte hastened to say he should not feel lonely in Denmark and touched his hand gently and sympathetically.

In fact, Carlos realized he had not said anything about

being lonely in Denmark. Danish—the difficult language. He remembered now that it was not called "alone" but "divorced."

"I've gotten divorced," he said.

Charlotte was perplexed. Here Carlos was saying he was no longer attached to anyone. He had to know she still felt the same about him as in the language school. She laid her hand on his, saying, "What can I do for you?"

Under no circumstances did Carlos want to arouse pity. But it felt good, almost healing, to suddenly touch the skin of a woman's hand again. Since Mette, he had been without the energy to get involved in a new relationship. And Charlotte was rather cute, yes, even beautiful. Why hadn't he noticed before?

Carlos squeezed Charlotte's hand, and she squeezed back. And in this silent and touching moment, Magasin's cafeteria became everybody else's world…and they were in its midst, the only foreigners, seeking the depths in each other's eyes.

Things went quickly after that. A short time later in Carlos's apartment in Nørrebro, they reached an orgasm with an intensity that surprised them both.

Afterwards they enjoyed gazing at each other's nakedness while they drank wine and smoked cigarettes like two people who were used to finding a way of relaxing after sex.

Charlotte broke the drowsy silence by casually saying; "Sometimes it was difficult for me to hide it from the others in the class."

What on earth did she mean? A bit confused, he smiled and pretended an understanding he did not have in the least.

She blushed a little. "There were days when I couldn't bear it…when you looked at me."

Carlos held her gaze and tried to figure things out. For some reason or other, she imagined that he had been interested in her when he was her student. But why spoil such a wonderful mood?

"It was difficult, very difficult for me, too," he said softly.

She got up, gave him a long kiss, and said one of the most difficult things she had ever said, "I have to hurry. My husband gets home soon."

When she had dressed, she worked up the courage to ask, "Would you like to meet again?"

Carlos nodded his assent.

Alone in his apartment, Carlos thought things over. He could recall situations where he and the teacher Charlotte had exchanged smiles, even laughed together, but that was all. Where she got these absurd thoughts about having something together in school, Carlos did not know. Back then there was no one in his life but Mette. But anyway, he was glad that he had been quick-witted enough to pretend and had immediately voiced the opposite of the truth. She had clearly been pleased with the little white lie, which in a magical way elevated their affair to the culmination of a logical development. Good. He went over to his glass of wine as he lit another cigarette.

The next time they were together, it went just as beautifully. So…there they sat facing each other in the room, drinking wine, smoking cigarettes, and enjoying the beautiful minutes following intercourse. And again Charlotte broke the comfortable silence.

She asked, "Why did you divorce Mette?"

Carlos had no real desire to pick at his wound. Yet, on the other hand, she was owed some kind of explanation. He found the postcard and showed it to her. And he could not avoid sounding melancholy when he said, "It was because of this."

Confused, Charlotte looked at the small piece of cardboard: the cause of Carlos's divorce. It took a few seconds before she felt the shock—she was holding the postcard she had sent him from the main station—and which she had completely forgotten.

"It came through the mail slot one day, and it destroyed my relationship."

"I don't understand," she said, seeking to conceal an increasing discomfort.

"I don't know who sent it...nor why, either. But Mette thought I had a relationship with another woman." And, not without difficulty, Carlos unfolded the whole painful story.

Charlotte felt an intense urge to put on her clothes. Nakedness had suddenly become burdensome. But her clothes were spread out all across the floor, and she could not let herself interrupt Carlos, who was struggling with his confession.

Later, when Charlotte sat in her car about to go home, she decided never ever to tell Carlos the truth about the postcard. Surely he had been interested in her during the course, but it was clear he simultaneously had strong feelings for Mette. And by sending the postcard, she had quite simply wrecked their relationship. A tinge of guilt touched her. But if their relationship was destroyed by an innocent piece of cardboard ...well, then, it could not have been worth very much, either.

Besides, at the moment when she had sent the postcard, she couldn't possibly have foreseen the consequences. In any case...Carlos would never know. Good. She started the car and followed the usual route home to her husband.

This part of the story where Carlos and Charlotte give themselves to each other, and slowly but surely consolidate their relationship, will be told quickly.

One can say that they kept on having good orgasms together in the apartment in Nørrebro. Which resulted in their need for each other becoming so urgent, and the pain of not seeing each other so unbearable, that they decided Charlotte should get a divorce so she could live with Carlos.

Charlotte got divorced. And they were truly happy that

sunny morning when they moved into an apartment in a well-to-do district of northern Sjælland.

One could correctly postulate that a postcard—in itself nothing but a piece of cardboard—contributed in the utmost to bringing Chilean Carlos and Danish Charlotte together.

And that is why it is quite tempting to let the story end here. Undeniably, there is a certain charm in the way they found each other.

But such an ending would neglect Peter, Charlotte's husband, a man with surprising resources, about whom very little has been said. At this point in the story, it would be interesting to know how he reacted to the harsh fact that his beloved wife abandoned him and the children in favor of a dark-skinned, salsa-dancing South American ten years her junior.

In order to continue the story (which, as mentioned, could easily end here), one has to go back in time to that point when Charlotte came home from Carlos and let Peter know that she was hopelessly in love with another man, a man she had been seeing frequently during the past three months. She wanted, and had to get, a divorce.

Peter's eyes filled with tears. He had known Charlotte for more than twenty years and was sure she meant every word. He sat down and wept.

Charlotte looked at the man who had been her husband for an eternity and discovered how unpleasant the mixture of pity and contempt could be.

"Why are you leaving me? You know that I love you!"

Charlotte sighed. There was so much Peter couldn't understand. That his love was not enough to keep her with him. That his love did not obligate her any more. That she had simply gotten tired of being loved by him. She did not say anything.

"Who is he?"

She made another discovery: it would have been much

easier if now she could describe a Dane about her same age. She drew a deep breath, told him who it was, and awaited Peter's reaction.

But no reaction came to this sensitive information. Race, culture, and age were at that moment empty concepts. Peter, the owner of several well-functioning companies, put his face in his hands and continued weeping.

The day after, they had a talk. Peter understood that she needed some time with her new man. So he had no objection to keeping the children, on the contrary. In this new situation where Charlotte was going through such a demanding change, she shouldn't be bothered with anything. She would be able to see the children whenever and wherever she wanted.

Moreover, Peter made it clear that he did not consider an apartment in Nørrebro a suitable place to live. She could simply rent or buy an apartment in northern Sjælland, the area where she belonged socially, and this was an expense that naturally was incumbent upon him. This way she could easily get by on her teaching salary. Furthermore, and so she should not be in any doubt about his positive attitude toward her new life, he was presenting her a nest egg of 50,000 kroner. And when he put the check on the table, he said, "It might be a good idea if you and your new boy friend take a vacation. That way you can get to know each other better."

Charlotte looked at him for a long while, and wishing to shake him up, she said, "I want to make it clear that I'm never coming back to you. Never."

Peter swallowed and bit his lip. Then he said softly, but stressing each word, "I'm doing it because I love you. Because I want the best for you."

"Even though I'm with another man?"

"Yes," Peter said after a painful silence. "I will always love you...even though you are with another man."

A few hours later, out in working-class Nørrebro, Carlos stared in disbelief at the check.

"What kind of a man is he?" he asked, shaking his head.

"Peter…well, that's the way he is."

"I won't take his money," he said, decisively.

"It isn't his money. It's my money now."

"Charlotte…! Neither you nor I will use your husband's money!"

"Stop it, Carlos! This is small change to Peter. I've told you that. He has tons of money."

This argument broke down Carlos's resistance. The money meant something to him if it meant something to the giver. But if it were a mere pittance to Peter, well, then, his pride was not wounded. Strange, but that is the way it felt. Yes…the hell with Peter's money.

"Where should we go?" Charlotte asked and took a stack of brochures out of her purse. She kissed him and added, "Just as long as I'm with you, I don't care where I am. But Greece is beautiful this time of year."

The day before they were to go, Peter gave Charlotte some expensive gifts. One was an intimate piece of underclothing, a teddy. The other was a pair of sunglasses—for Carlos.

Carlos was struck dumb when he saw the exquisite teddy. But when it came to the designer sunglasses, his gift, he nearly went into shock.

"What am I supposed to do with these?" he mumbled.

"Just put them on," Charlotte answered cheerfully.

"Fine," he said in a rage. "You wear his teddy, and I put on the sunglasses. What the hell is he up to?"

"He isn't up to anything," Charlotte laughed again. "That's just the way he is."

"The way he is…" thought Carlos. "What kind of way is that? I've literally taken his wife, and here we get a vacation and strange gifts."

Carlos considered the matter further. If he demanded that the gifts be thrown away, Charlotte could easily interpret it as a sign of jealousy. He tried to be honest with himself and acknowledge a possible jealousy.

And he reached the conclusion that if he had nothing against conceding a possible jealousy, it was most likely because there was not any. But why did the gifts upset him so? He did not know. "Well…fuck Peter and his gifts!"

On the little Greek island chosen by Charlotte, they floated on an endless high. They danced every evening at a salsa discothèque for tourist groups, where Carlos attracted a lot of attention because of his impressive mastery of extraordinary dance steps. They talked late into the night and became absorbed in each other's lives and feelings. They had sex frequently—on the beach, in the rented car, in the fields, wherever they could do it.

The last night on the island they drank a great deal. And when they were at the peak of their love-making, on a mattress on the balcony, Carlos suddenly stopped—and pulled out of her. He went into their room, and when he came back, he was wearing Peter's gift, the sunglasses. He threw the teddy at her.

"No, Carlos. You don't mean it," Charlotte said.

"Hurry up," Carlos answered behind the sunglasses.

A second before he reached his climax, he pulled out of her again. The next second he ejaculated on the part of the teddy that covered her buttocks and back.

Afterwards they lay on the mattress. He behind the sunglasses and she in the soiled teddy. They drank wine, smoked, and laughed. And even though it was not said, both of them knew that in some way or other they were laughing at Peter.

Shortly after the plane took off and found its course toward Copenhagen, it struck Carlos that he had spent fourteen days in...Greece! And he remembered that after Mette's confession about a whole week with a Greek in Greece, everything related to Greeks and Greece pained him.

And, incredibly, during his stay on the island he had not given a single thought to either Mette or her Greek. He kissed Charlotte, held her hand, closed his eyes, and didn't wake until the plane approached Kastrup airport.

Carlos wore his sunglasses and looked like the epitome of a charter tourist when, on the way out of customs in Kastrup, he saw a man approach them with an obliging smile. Before he had a chance to react, the elegant man kissed Charlotte on the cheek and stretched out his hand toward him. Astonished, he shook the man's hand.

"Hi. Nice to meet you, Carlos," the man said amicably. "I'm Peter."

Peter had come out to the airport in order to drive them home to Nørrebro. On the way, he told them that everything was arranged about the apartment, which Charlotte—and of course, Carlos as well—would soon move into.

The car reached Nørrebro. And it occurred to Carlos that he was wearing Peter's sunglasses. He felt extremely awkward without knowing exactly why. Reluctantly, he said, "Thanks for the glasses, Peter."

"Well," Peter answered and shrugged his shoulders, "they look great on you."

"What kind of a man is he?" Carlos asked himself again.

Charlotte and Carlos moved in together. Carlos did not want to move into an apartment Peter was paying for. He brought all his clothes and, as it was, he lived there, but he didn't give up his own apartment, which he sublet to another Chilean who was working without a residency permit.

During the following months their relationship was like a new dimension owned solely by them. They looked back on their former lives with a certain disdain. She distanced herself from her old friends, who now seemed bourgeois and uninteresting. And he thought his Latin American friends' class and life style were not in harmony with his new way of living. To have each other was enough for Charlotte and Carlos.

At this point of the story, just when everything seems to be so fine and beautiful, the trail we leave, the chain of events that we call the past, begins to catch up with Carlos and Charlotte in the most capricious way.

When Carlos and Mette had split up, his family, at home in the dusty village in northern Chile, thought that it would be good for him to come back for a visit.

The Chilean desert's clear light, the old British buildings from the mining days, childhood friends—everything Carlos grew up with—would help him to cope with a new life. He had seemed somewhat depressed in his letters and on the telephone, alone and faraway in chilly Denmark. The family put their solidarity into action. They worked hard, saved money, and eventually sent Carlos a ticket so he could spend the next Christmas and New Year's in the bosom of the family.

Time went by faster than usual, and suddenly there were only three weeks until the trip to Chile. Carlos realized that unconsciously he had put off mentioning or making a decision about the trip. Because how could he show up at home with a woman ten years older than himself...and who had two children?

In Chile everything is permitted as long as you maintain an unassailable moral façade. Chileans, most of them anyway, live completely by the principle: morality is good, but double morality is twice as good. It would, for example, be perfectly acceptable if he was married to a woman of his own age and enjoyed himself with a ten-year-older lover. But here he came with a divorced mother, forty years old, with whom he had cohabited—and that was something entirely different, something that quite definitely fell outside the guidelines.

These thoughts defined an unbridgeable chasm between Denmark and Chile. The Danes make a supreme effort to show respect for the private lives of others, and their mutual discretion and good upbringing make them even more vulnerable. They need to have crisis intervention for things that a Chilean would forget in a few hours. Chileans are thick-skinned; their society is just as inconsiderate as the way they say things to each other. And on top of that they are tactless and think they have the right to meddle in other people's private affairs.

It seemed as if the worst situations could occur. His mother dropping a remark that "Such a relationship can't last long for obvious reasons..." Or "...she seems very sweet, but unfortunately it's well-known that women, especially mothers, who go after young men are loose in virtue." His brother, or a good friend might ask, "Is there something quite special she does (in bed, is understood) that keeps you from the young Danish beauties...?" Charlotte didn't understand Spanish well, but there are certain things you don't need language to comprehend.

He loved his family and valued his friends. Good people, they were. To try to change them was as impossible as trying to change all of Chile. But if they ended up hurting Charlotte, then he would be compelled, even against his will, to tell them a few truths: that they were hypocritical, small-minded, provincial, and things a lot worse. And to what good? It would all just end up with a lot of wounded people.

Carlos needed to find an answer to his dilemma. There was no way to cancel the trip and disappoint his whole family, who had slaved and saved to bring him home. There was nothing he would rather do than go to Chile with Charlotte and show her everything that had been his life before Denmark. But she simply could not come along when his family would be the setting for the visit. Why on earth could things not fit together? Life was hard and illogical, Carlos thought.

One night, a drunk and confused Carlos, lurching from bar to bar in Copenhagen, saw, as if in a vision, exactly what he needed to see: he would go to Chile—without Charlotte.

Less than an hour later, he sat across from Charlotte in their bed and explained that he would travel to Chile in ten days—alone.

Charlotte, who had just been awakened and had never seen him so drunk, not even in Greece, yawned and asked, "Without me…why?"

But Carlos had not given a thought to what reason he should give for traveling alone. He stopped and just looked at her, unable to say a word. And in the middle of the chaos that grew inside his head, only one comprehensible fact stood out—that he was very drunk.

"Carlos… Why should you suddenly travel to Chile alone…?"

Finally he said, "I'm going alone." And added, "There's nothing more to discuss."

The days passed and the time for the trip drew near. And the happiness that Charlotte and Carlos had built together began to crack and splinter.

Charlotte's initial surprise changed quickly into a mixture of suspicion and anger. Perhaps he was taking another woman to Chile. Maybe criminal activity was the reason for the trip, narcotics, or something like that. Maybe he had a wife and five children in his homeland, just like some other immigrants, who nevertheless enjoyed entertaining themselves with Danish women. Maybe he would leave, never to return. Why had he turned so strange? Suddenly it was an entirely different Carlos she lived with.

Carlos saw with desperation that no matter what he said, the truth or lies, or whether he kept silent, the situation grew worse minute by minute. How could he have been so stupid?

He had always had bad luck with fantastic ideas that showed up during a drinking spree.

They spoke only when it was absolutely necessary. And like a campfire in the rain, their formerly inspirational sex life went out.

Finally Carlos decided to reveal the real reason for traveling to Chile alone. Otherwise, Charlotte could end up thinking he had a wife and five children in Chile or was a courier for a narcotics ring. His silence had really wounded her. Still he was afraid the truth might very well be much more cruel than silence.

It is difficult to say whether he chose the very last moment...or if it was his confused condition that chose it for him. He had just ordered the taxi for the airport when he began to speak out.

Charlotte listened without saying a word. When the taxi came, Carlos had finished with the gist of his explanation: his family's likely reaction to her age. He tried to kiss her goodbye, but she turned her face away. While the taxi honked outside, he tried in vain to embrace her, but her body was like stone, hard and cold. She did not turn her face toward the door until he had closed it behind him.

Back in the old country, which had seen his birth and growth to manhood, Carlos nearly went out of his mind. Neither family, friends, nor his childhood landscape could make him the least bit happy. He tried a number of times to contact Charlotte in Denmark. But the few times the telephone was lifted at the other end and he said hello, it was immediately hung up. And he stood there holding a hopeless plastic device that mocked him with an endless dut-dut. What was he doing in this hole of a city in the middle of the world's most merciless desert? Why did his family and friends try to make him happy all the time? Why was Charlotte so far away that he could not talk with her? Everything around Carlos was falling apart.

The days crept by, one after the other, like steps down a stairway to Hell itself. When he was not sad and withdrawn, he was fairly drunk and behaved crudely and offensively toward everything and everyone. He kept on telephoning, but the receiver was always hung up.

Then it happened. A week before his return to Denmark he called from a telephone booth, said hello, and Charlotte's voice answered hello from the other side of the globe. He immediately became both sober and stunned. Her voice was a caress that had returned to him. He lit a cigarette.

"What do you want," Charlotte asked.

"I miss you," he said sincerely.

"Why are you calling?"

"Why? Because I want to know how you are." He shouted, "Three weeks have gone by!" Then he paused and lowered his voice, "Three weeks…"

"I'm in the middle of packing your things up. I'll send them to your Chilean friend who's living in your apartment." Then she added, "I'm moving back in with Peter."

"What are you saying?" He had heard it, but hoped he would hear something entirely different if he asked again.

Charlotte repeated, "I'm moving back in with Peter."

Carlos dropped the telephone, which fell and dangled like an executed man at a hanging. Slowly, like a gigantic carousel, his hometown, the surrounding desert, and the whole world began rotating around him. He sat down on the ground and tossed his cigarette away. A terrible urge to vomit crawled up from his stomach, and he remembered that at some place or other, in Chile, or maybe in Denmark, he had heard someone say that life's hardest blows have a habit of hitting when you least expect them. Charlotte was back with the man whom they had laughed at together. Now Charlotte and Peter were laughing at him.

Thousands of miles away in northern Sjælland, Charlotte

hung up the phone and kept her eyes on it for a few seconds; then she looked up.

There was the bedroom she had shared with Carlos and where Peter was now busy stuffing Carlos's things into packing boxes. Peter had taken the unpleasant work upon himself because she herself did not have the energy for it. He would never do anything to hurt her in any way. Because he really loved her. She lit a cigarette. To be able to count on another person's love meant everything in life. Strange that she had to undergo so much in order to see it.

She was about to put out the cigarette when the telephone rang. She picked up and said hello. "You can't move back to Peter again!" Carlos's voice shouted.

"And why can't I?" she said in a challenging tone.

"What the hell kind of way is that to talk!" Carlos shouted. He stopped and took a deep breath. He really wanted to control himself. "We haven't talked with each other. You can't just move back to him!"

She answered with the same tone. "We're packing your things right now."

"We? Why is he in our home?" he asked, incredulous.

"He's helping me to pack your things. You shouldn't count on this apartment any more. Peter's selling it."

Now Carlos shouted again, "Why are you moving back to him? For Christ's sake, can't you get along without his money? Or what?"

"You're having a good time in Chile with your family, aren't you?"

"Have you been to bed with him? Have you?!"

"I'm telling you I'm moving back in with him. That answer will have to be enough."

"You filthy whore. You...you..." Rage kept him from remembering more Danish swear words. He wanted to call her every horrible thing he could imagine in Spanish, but that would only worsen the situation, his situation. Peter?!

Just because he went to Chile alone. Shouldn't it take more than that to make her go back to Peter?

"Whore!" he shouted with the full force of his lungs. "Whore!" And then he hung up.

Charlotte hung up, too. She lit another cigarette, went to the living room, and poured a glass of cognac. "Whore…" Some words were worse than knives.

Peter, who had heard the discussion from the bedroom, came over to her and asked, "How are you, sweetheart?"

"Not so good," Charlotte answered.

"Carlos won't understand," he said thoughtfully. Charlotte didn't answer.

"Well," he added, "It's hard, something like this." And he went into the bedroom and continued stuffing Carlos's things into the packing cases.

Was she a whore because she had felt lonely and humiliated while Carlos preferred to be with his family in Chile? Was she a whore because she had gone back to her husband?

Charlotte was about to pour herself another glass of cognac when the telephone rang again. It could only be Carlos.

Peter came into the room. "Sweetheart," he said, concerned, "maybe I can get him to understand that it's finished between you two. He isn't stupid, after all. He's just finding it difficult to accept the situation."

Charlotte didn't listen to Peter and lifted the receiver. Carlos's agitated breathing came through the phone right into her eardrum. She couldn't help but remember some of their sexual highs. Glimpses of the first time they were together in Nørrebro and in Greece assaulted her. But she closed her eyes and pushed these now inappropriate memories out of her mind.

At last Carlos spoke, "Now I'll tell you something, you whore!"

She did not open her eyes; on the contrary, she shut them

even tighter. Peter tactfully disappeared into the bedroom again.

Carlos continued, "That time at evening school—you can remember that all right, can't you? Nothing was as you thought it was in your cheap fantasy. And do you know what…?"

Charlotte did not want to hear any more. An indefinable chill gripped her heart. Carlos had certainly disappointed and humiliated her. But that time when she had dreamed about him still lay inside her heart, untouched, like an inner proof that it was still possible to find and experience love in a pure state. If that, too, were lost…then the emptiness that afflicted her now would be intolerable.

"And you know what…?!"

She heard a voice full of destructiveness. And everything told her that it was best to hang up. She felt she was falling into a void when she said, "Say whatever you want, Carlos."

"I lied the first time we were together in my apartment. While we were in evening school, I never thought about you except as a boring old schoolteacher!"

Carlos knew very well it was wrong, no matter what, to say something so hurtful. But Peter…How could she let herself be screwed by Peter?

"Why are you saying that?" Charlotte said, breaking into tears. He had destroyed the only beautiful thing she had left from their relationship—the time at the evening school. She didn't hang up because perhaps he would say he did not mean it. Only his agitated breathing came through.

For Carlos it was not a question of true or false, but of getting even. He said, "You were an old, superannuated rich man's wife in fashionable schoolgirl clothes. I was in love with Mette. And you were nothing, nothing! Compared to her!"

Charlotte woke. Suddenly it was not a singular and marvelous experience he was killing in her. He was degrading her in comparison to his earlier woman. A cold breath ran through her veins. She dried her tears and coughed to clear her throat.

He said, "Mette was young and beautiful." Then he shouted, "And you are a pathetic hag compared to her!"

This last remark made her even colder, stronger. "Carlos…" she said slowly and deliberately, "It's really too bad that your relationship with Mette went to pieces over a postcard. I really feel for you." And then she said with an exaggerated clarity, exactly as when she used to teach him Danish, "You stupid Chilean, you had seen my handwriting a million times and you still couldn't figure it out…I was the one who sent you the postcard."

It got absolutely quiet over the line. Even his breathing was gone. She waited.

"You…you sent the postcard…?"

"Yes, Carlos, I sent you the postcard!" She hung up and pulled out the telephone plug. Then she lit another cigarette and went out onto the balcony. It was cold. But the cold she felt within her was worse than any Danish winter.

Carlos looked toward the road that led out of the city, out toward the desert and the gigantic copper-colored mountains. Once more the sun burned the gold and arid landscape. He badly needed to walk and walk until the pain and the devastating sun changed him to desert dust forever.

From the bedroom, Peter observed Charlotte on the balcony. It was clear she needed to be alone with her thoughts. On the other hand, it was a cold evening, and if she didn't come in herself after a few minutes, he would go out and bring her back into the living room.

Peter took a deep breath and closed his eyes. In this happy moment, his soul filled with warmth, and tears of happiness ran slowly down his cheeks. For many months he had wandered about through subterranean holes like a rat, alone and lonesome. And now he had come up to the surface, up to Charlotte.

Peter had always known he was not the kind of exciting

man whom Charlotte had often dreamed about. Therefore, when Carlos came into the picture, Peter was crushed—but not really surprised.

Well…he was not dark-haired, did not talk with a charming accent, and absolutely could not dance the salsa. But he was able to love her with his whole heart. And love was the most important, most beautiful thing in the world. So many stupid people who thought that money could buy happiness envied him because he was rich. But money had not brought Charlotte back to him. She was back with him because Carlos had failed her and caused her pain.

All of Carlos's clothes were packed. Now it was his books' turn to disappear down into the packing case. "Danish for Foreigners" was the title of one of the books. And Peter thought that perhaps, after a while, Charlotte would begin to fantasize about an exciting man again. There were, after all, exciting men everywhere. Perhaps next time it would be a Danish Carlos. All things considered, a new threatening Carlos could come from anywhere. And so what? He felt himself stronger than ever. For no Carlos would be able to love Charlotte as he did.

Peter dried the tears from his eyes. It was time to go out on the balcony and say to Charlotte, "Sweetheart, it's cold out there. Come in."

Just One Answer

The young man knocked on the door and waited anxiously. After a few seconds it occurred to him that perhaps no one would open the door...and so he would have to wait an eternity in the long dark corridor. He had to rest. He had to sleep. And Sandholm, Denmark's largest refugee camp, was his only chance tonight.

Finally the door opened and he breathed easier.

"Hello," he said in English to the African face that appeared before him.

"Hello," the African answered, confused.

The men looked at each other just to determine they had nothing to say to one another. The African instinctively stepped back from the door.

The young man walked into the room and shut the door behind him. With a single glance, he counted the men in the room: two Africans, two Arabs, and three East Europeans. The seven men were now observing him with cautious curiosity. He had come into the room without keys or bedclothes, and unescorted by the Red Cross attendants.

"Hello," he said, this time to everyone and to no one.

"Hello," some of the men answered, more out of obligation than hospitality.

The young man looked around. Right next to the window there was a free bed. He hurried over to it. The other men in the room returned to their own anxieties about the next day, when they were all going to be interviewed, through interpreters, by the Danish police.

He sat down on the bed and took off his jacket and shoes. Quickly he asked himself the usual question. Should he use his jacket to cover his body or as a pillow?

He lay down on his back, covering himself with the jacket and felt immediately a familiar fatigue inside his body. The outcome of 12 hours of work at Arden's Pizzeria always first appeared when he lay down.

The dim light of the room was reassuring. The other men didn't seem to give him a single thought. And why should they? They had the right to a bed and bedclothes. In the morning they would be interviewed by the police, and with a little luck—the luck he himself didn't have—they would be allowed to start a new life in Denmark.

The young man closed his eyes. It was centuries since he, too, had had the right to a bed, a blanket, and a pillow in Sandholm. He closed his eyes and let his mind dream and his body rest.

An unexpected sound woke him. The sound came from the door handle, and now he could hear a key being turned in the lock. The door opened, and two Red Cross attendants came in—a man and a woman. The man was dark-skinned, possibly a former refugee, one of the lucky ones who had succeeded in staying in Denmark. The woman was blond, Danish to the hilt. They seemed to fill up the whole room.

"Good evening, gentlemen," the dark-skinned man said in English and in the usual Red Cross tone, friendly but firm. He looked at a piece of paper he held in his hand and said, still in English, that as far as he could see, there was one man too many in the room.

The attendants looked at each man in the room, one after the other. Their gaze stopped as soon as they set eyes on him.

"Do you live in this camp?" the Danish woman asked.

The young man pushed his jacket aside and sat up on the edge of his bed. He rubbed his eyes to clear his sight but also to gain a few seconds time.

The dark-skinned attendant said, "My friend, you know the rules of the camp. You'll have to leave."

The young man knew the rules just as well as the two attendants. Sandholm was only for asylum-seekers in the Red Cross program whose requests for asylum were still pending.

He looked down at his feet, clad only in socks. He held

his head in both hands. Once, he too had been a new arrival, just as the other men in the room were now. By his second day he had already been interviewed by the Danish police, and had explained why he needed asylum in Denmark. But later, some of his countrymen who had already gotten asylum told him that everything he had said to the Danish police was precisely what you shouldn't say. So they recommended that next time he should say the opposite of what he had said in the first interview. And consequently, at the second interview he said the opposite of what he had said in the first one.

"Sorry. But you have to leave the camp..." said a distant voice.

But when he read the transcript of the first interview, he discovered that some of the things he had said had been recorded in an entirely different way. Therefore he had contradicted some things he had really never said at all. He thought that was probably the fault of his interpreter, who spoke his language but came from a different country. And then he happened to meet some entirely different countrymen, who had also received asylum in Denmark, and they explained to him that he should never change anything he had already said to the police because then they would think he had lied and for that reason alone would expel him from Denmark. So he went to the police and tried to get his story straight. But in the middle of his explanation, he got confused and suddenly couldn't remember what had happened and what hadn't happened, who had said one thing and who another, what came first and what came after. He signed yet another new declaration anyway. No one had pressured him to sign...but wasn't that what one always did after such an interview?

"Excuse me..." Yet another voice tried to reach him.

And now, three years later, yes, now three years later, he was about to be expelled from Denmark. How could that be when others from his country already had a nice place to live and were learning Danish?

"Sorry. But you have to leave the camp!" The Danish woman spoke louder now.

Finally the young man lifted his head and looked at the two night attendants.

They stood there in that incomprehensible Danish manner which let him understand clearly that even though they were throwing him out, they had nothing against him personally.

He coughed to clear his throat and try his luck. Then he told the attendants he didn't have enough money to get back to Copenhagen.

With a friendly smile the dark-skinned man responded that of course he had the money. He certainly hadn't come all the way out to Sandholm, far in the countryside, without enough money to get back.

But he insisted he didn't have the money. Some friends of his in Sandholm were going to lend him some in the morning.

The Danish woman said, also in an agreeable manner, that if he had friends in Sandholm, why was he sleeping here, in the room for new arrivals and not in his friends' room?

He was quick to answer that he hadn't seen his friends for a few weeks and so he didn't know which room they were in.

The dark-skinned men said that if he hadn't seen his friends in weeks, then how could he know they would lend him money in the morning?

He breathed a sigh of despair. These Red Cross people had heard all kinds of stories from people from every part of the world. They were always polite, but they would call the police if he refused to leave this room and Sandholm. And he had to avoid the police at all costs. Just the thought of going back to Copenhagen weighed down every part of his body. He got up, put on his jacket and shoes, picked up his bag, and left the room, escorted by the two attendants.

On the way toward the portal, he felt the night's refreshing air. They walked past the nurse's building, past the cafeteria, and the laundry room. It was very quiet. Sandholm and its nearly one thousand inhabitants from all over the world slept, as people sleep in every other quiet little city. On his very first day in Sandholm he had noticed this air—the purest air he had ever experienced anywhere. It was that summer day, his first day, when he, full of tension and hope, approached the large portal to seek asylum. A few days later the Red Cross lent him a bicycle so he could lose himself in the fields and woods around Sandholm. And the sun, the mild Danish sun, shone over it all—and he was happy and believed that all his future Danish summers would be the same.

They stopped when they reached the portal.

"Goodbye," said the dark-skinned man.

"And good luck," added the Danish woman. And it seemed as if she meant it.

The night attendants turned around and walked back through the portal again.

The young man stood at the bus stop just across from the entrance to Sandholm and saw that it would be 50 minutes before the next bus to Allerød showed up. What now? He fingered his bundle of keys and the temptation to go to the pizzeria to sleep was nearly overwhelming. But if Ardem found out he had slept at the store, it was the end of work for him. Ardem wouldn't allow a foreigner who lived illegally in Denmark to spend the night in his pizzeria. But Ardem had nothing against letting him work during the day even though that was even more illegal.

What about taking a chance—just for this one night? But what was he going to do without the little money he earned if Ardem fired him? But where would he sleep tonight? In an S-Train station? In a park? In a hallway? What about one of the all-night cafes in Copenhagen? And what would happen if the police arrested him late at night in a bar...or in a park?

And what about tomorrow if he didn't get any sleep—how would he get through the 12 hours at the pizzeria?

The mild night invited him to walk the nearly 40 minutes it would take to get to Allerød. But he was tired, more tired than he had ever been. He took a deep breath to clear his head and give himself the strength to make a decision.

The young man looked across at Sandholm's portal— once, three years ago, he had walked through it.

The huge spotlights at the portal broke the darkness and made the fence and the yellow buildings seem something from another world. Otherwise everything was dark and deserted in the enormous loneliness around him. But he knew that at daybreak the sky, the fields, the trees and bushes would live as if they were forms and colors in a newly painted picture.

Through the long winter he had looked forward to the summer—because the Danish summer was not as a summer should be…and yet it was so green and so beautiful. But his days in Denmark were numbered. And he had no place to go. His countrymen here in Denmark didn't have time to help him. Sooner or later the police would catch him. And he would be deported to his own country—a place to which he could not return.

His savings should be enough to buy a forged passport and a ticket to Germany. Or maybe to Sweden or Poland. But…with the bad luck that plagued him, it was impossible to know which was the right choice.

He began to walk towards Allerød. And when he crossed the wide King's Road and reached the woods, he asked himself…How could this possibly be his last summer in Denmark? He stopped. The darkness of the wood was thick and he could barely see his hands. How could it be? His first two days in Denmark he had cycled through this very same place. And the wood and its magnificence had welcomed him. Now he was leaving Denmark. And he felt like nothing on the way to nothing. No one would miss, much less remember him, in this country from which he had expected everything. He looked up at the sky and let his eyes glide over the thousands of stars above. And again he came to the conclusion that there was only one answer to it all—he was unlucky…very unlucky.

The young man looked toward the road that farther down freed itself from the wood and turned toward Allerød. He had to hurry to the station…otherwise he would miss the last train to Copenhagen.

Adam and Shaha

There were four men and a woman, the drunk and boisterous Finns around the only table in the room. And they fell silent, as if they had seen a ghost, when the dark-skinned, longhaired man with Indian features came in from the hallway.

Adán Aculefu, a 22-year-old Chilean, born in the city of Temuco, walked into the room, where bountiful warmth greeted him. The attention he used to attract in Denmark was nothing compared to what he caused here in Finland. He nodded toward the table and said, "Hello."

One of the Finns, the woman, answered something or other, possibly in Finnish. The other haggard faces remained a big question mark as a cautious Adán chose the bed farthest from their table.

With a tired gesture, Adán tossed his bundle of disposable bedclothes on the metallic bunk bed. He let his bag glide from his shoulder until it landed on the floor, and he took off his winter coat. He heaved a weary sigh…well, finally, he was in Finland. In fact, he had already been in Finland for several hours since his arrival from Sweden to the Finnish port city of Turku.

And perhaps it was this humble and waiting bed in a locker room in Olympia Stadium that convinced him his long journey had ended. Just two days separated him from New Year's Eve. The fact that he had traveled all the way from Århus to this place to wait for 1976 to become 1977 seemed an incomprehensible absurdity. Would Finland be the far away place he needed? Would he find the clarity he sought?

The Finns drifted back to their noisy conversation. A bottle of liquor circulated among them with quick, furtive movements. Certainly the bottle had to be kept hidden from the attendant on duty, who was stationed in the office at the entrance to the stadium.

The metal bed gave a creaking whine when it received

him. Some few lamps set in the walls bathed everything in a faded, indifferent light—the noisy Finns, the empty beds, the open and deserted lockers. To the right, at the beginning of a long and dim corridor, there was a shower room. Yes, he was a long way from Århus and Grøfthøj Park, where Bettina and Blanca, each in her own concrete apartment house and each in her own loneliness, thought of him—while he lay on a rickety bed in a soccer stadium locker room which had been converted into a hostel…in Finland.

Adán took his notebook from his shoulder bag and read the poem he had written since his departure from Århus. The four last lines read:

El amor es tantas, tantas cosas
(Love is so many, many things)

que yo nunca las encontraré todas
(that I'll never be able to find them all)

Quién tiene un corazón tan grande y fuerte
(who has a heart so big and so strong)

para amar a dos personas…sin quebrarse él mismo en
dos?
(to love two people…without splitting himself in two?)

Adán could still recognize the feelings behind these words written in the train between Turku and Helsinki. It took him a fairly long time to write a single line, but he was always satisfied. For every line he wrote was a little piece of truth that brought him closer to himself. The opposite of life—which forced him to lie, to flee from his own feelings. Damn! And what else could he have done? Adán's empty eyes gazed back into the past. The informer, one of those socialist, revolutionary "comrades." What did the stool pigeon get for his information? February 1974…a squad of soldiers grabbed him at home on the outskirts of Temuco, his native town in southern Chile. Blanca comes out of her parents' house crying, tries to keep the soldiers from hauling him off, but they shove her away. Prison—torture, degradation, months and months in an indescribable hell. Only the thought of seeing Blanca and his family again keeps him going. August 1974—the order of expulsion from the land his forefathers had lived on for centuries before the Spanish came. Denmark—an airport and a bus waiting for him and another Chilean who came on the same flight. Grøfthøj Park—a handful of Chileans welcome him. "Comrade"...he hates that word—any traitor can hide behind it. The Danes—these incredible people who send him to the doctor, to the dentist, to the psychologist, and heal what the Chileans had destroyed in him. And the neighbors, the Danish neighbors give a welcome party for the Chileans, and because it is impossible to buy a Chilean flag in Denmark, they sew one themselves where the red and blue colors are reversed. A joyous party: people want to get to know each other. But he misses Blanca. And Bettina, the girl living in Grøfthøj Park's highest building, approaches him, smiling. Adán blinked a few times to adjust his sight to the present, to the locker room in Olympia Stadium, where the Finns now seemed used to his presence. After some time, the following lines were added to the poem in his notebook:

Los rostros del amor aparecen y desaparecen—el uno en
el otro
(The faces of love appear and disappear—the one in the
other)

mientras mi echar de menos es como mi culpa—un
abismo
(while my need is like my guilt—an abyss)

que crece dentro y fuera de mí
(growing inside and outside of me)

He put the notebook on the bed without closing it. Maybe it was time to take a long shower.

The stinging and restorative blows of water made him relax and close his eyes, Grøfthøj Park... Again he saw the green and well-ordered Grøfthøj Park, his first Denmark, his first life after prison. He slept every night with Bettina, who knew about Blanca, but nevertheless was loving and helped him get acclimated. And Blanca—shortly after he was arrested, her whole family had moved to another city. And he went to Denmark without seeing her again. His time with Bettina in Grøfthøj Park went along peacefully until the letter from Blanca arrived and changed everything. For she had searched for him and now knew he was in Denmark. She still loved him. And from the moment he opened the letter, the chasm beneath his feet began to widen.

Adán turned up the hot water and stood there with closed eyes. If only one of them were there, either Bettina or Blanca, but both of them were there, not far from each other in Grøfthøj Park. Was it all his damn fault? When the letter came, he told Bettina that he had to bring Blanca to Denmark. Bettina looked up at the sky and then at him—her face was bathed in tears. Still they went on seeing each other and sleeping together. It took months to marry Blanca through a power of attorney, and several months more to get her to Denmark. And just two weeks ago, Blanca walked into his apartment in Grøfthøj Park. They had not seen each other since his arrest nearly two years earlier. And it was still the same Blanca, but in the meantime he had changed. And he also loved Bettina, with whom he had shared his life for more than a year. Adán had to choose, but he could not. He went from one to the other, and every time brought more pain to them and to himself. Christmas Eve he went to Copenhagen.

Being with one of them was a betrayal of the other. Just the thought of spending New Year's Eve with one while the other was miserable made him sick. Desperate, faced with an impossible choice that split him internally, he decided to go to Finland, a country that was far distant on the atlas when he was a happy schoolboy in Temuco. No, there was nothing else he could have done.

He turned off the water and was suddenly struck by the sense that something around him was missing. It was the chatter of the Finns—he couldn't hear it any more. He put his clothes on hurriedly and went out into the hallway from where he could see their table. They were silent, disconcerted, as they stared in the direction of his bed. Adán went into the locker room, and there he saw a dark-haired, thin man in a thin gray suit who stood observing his bed. He had a coat over his right arm; in his left hand he held a suitcase. His shoes were soaked through from the slush outside. Where in the world was he from? And why was he particularly interested in his bed?

Adán approached until the strange man turned around. The man's skin color reminded him of the Indian-Ugandan refugees who lived in Grøfthøj Park. But the eyes, the facial features, the shiny oiled hair, the screaming-red tie, and the indefinable but heavy scent of perfume—no, Adán had never before seen anything like that. He guessed the man to be about his own age. The man was obviously surprised by Adán's appearance, as Adán was by his. He asked in a mild, polite voice, in English, "Is this your bed?"

"Yes," Adán answered. His coat, wool sweater, and open notebook lay on the bed and the shoulder bag beside it on the floor. And the strange man still couldn't see that the bed was taken?

"Sorry," the man said. And added nervously, nearly fearfully, "I'm so sorry."

"No problem," Adán answered.

And the strange man went over to an unoccupied bed.

"Well…" Adán thought, still puzzled. Now he might just as well go to bed. The Finns were probably homeless or something. They had already turned in. The strange thin man walked toward the shower room with a towel and a lot of other things in his hands. Their eyes met a second. Strange, but Finland and the Finns suddenly provided them with good reason to feel they had a lot in common. Adán would try to get to sleep and forget why he found himself in Finland. Fatigue was overtaking his whole body. Maybe he would be lucky tonight and fall asleep quickly.

At exactly eight o'clock the attendant on duty, an older, white-haired man, banged on one of the steel bed frames with a pipe and woke the five Finns and the Chilean and the strange man. The Finns bellyached, but the message was relentless. The hostel closed in a few minutes and reopened again at eight P.M. Anyone planning to return in the evening could store his belongings in one of the lockers. Adán dressed quickly. A Finland under daylight awaited him outside.

An overwhelming white world met him. The snow pushed everything else into the background. It was heavier and thicker than in Denmark, and the light it reflected hurt his eyes. He took some slippery steps in the direction of the trolley stop and the road to Helsinki. He stopped and turned all the way around a couple of times while he felt a strong urge to shout something or other at the wild and redeeming landscape. But he was not the one who shouted. "Hi! Hi!" he heard and then caught sight of the strange man from the hostel approaching him from the snow-covered path. Adán nearly thought it was some kind of vision. The lean man in the thin clothes—in that weather!

"I'm from Bangladesh," the man said and smiled. "And you?"

Adán was thankful for the broken English he had learned in language school in Århus, and, still a little surprised, he answered the question.

"Chilean?" The strange man's face lit up. 'You're a real Chilean—like Neruda?"

Adán was speechless. Here in the midst of the Finnish snow this man from Bangladesh was asking if he were a real Chilean like Neruda!

"I love Neruda!" the man from Bangladesh said with eyes that expected his enthusiasm to be returned.

"Yes," Adán said, at a loss for something better, "I'm a Chilean, like Neruda." And he wondered momentarily if this man from Bangladesh had ever heard Neruda's monotonous and tiresome voice.

The man added that he had studied literature at the university in Dacca, which Adán guessed must be an important city in Bangladesh.

"My name is Shaha _ _ _ _ ," he said and put out his hand.

Adán, who only understood the first half of the name, Shaha, shook hands and introduced himself. Then, without further ceremony, Shaha said he knew a good place to get breakfast. His teeth chattered and he rubbed his hands to generate a little warmth. "I really love Neruda," he said with conviction as they climbed aboard the trolley.

Adán could not care less about Neruda, or about any other poet for that matter. And he cared even less for this unexpected company. It was precisely because he wanted to be alone that he had gone to Finland.

After 15 minutes in the trolley, they sat in a small café in Helsinki's main railway station. From time to time, everyone there looked at them—the only dark faces in the whole café. According to Shaha, who knew the city well, they were in the cheapest café in Helsinki. Adán bought an inexpensive breakfast combo consisting of bread, coffee, and cheese. Shaha launched his day with something completely different—hot chocolate and French fries bathed in ketchup, which did not exactly diminish the attention of the other customers in the café.

Adán compared everything to Denmark—and everything, including the people, seemed colorless and strange in an inexplicable way. A year and a half in Århus had made Denmark his home. His thoughts flew toward Grøfthøj Park—and to Blanca and Bettina.

Suddenly Shaha asked, "Adam, do you know why I'm in Finland?"

"Adam…" His name was Adán with the accent on the last syllable, and every time he introduced himself, he pronounced it as clearly as he could. He shrugged his shoulders in reply. And Shaha began to answer his own question…some months ago in Dacca, Shaha had fallen in love with a Finnish girl who was visiting his country on an aid program. The attempts of his family to get him married had failed so far—Bangladeshi girls just did not interest him. The Finnish girl was the only one for him. Day after day, Shaha dreamed about her until one day he confessed his love. She smiled and gave him a kiss on the cheek. The night before she left for Finland, they slept together, which for Shaha was an incontrovertible sign that her love for him was just as great as his love for her. However, for some reason or other, she never answered the many letters he sent her afterward. Desperate, Shaha stole a great deal of money from his father, bought an airline ticket, and flew to Finland.

"Adam," Shaha said. "I did a terrible thing. I'm so ashamed."

"Adam" again. Adán had given up trying to correct the mistake. Shaha continued: Yes…he would never be able to look his father in the eye again. Arriving in Helsinki, he took a taxi from the airport to her address. When she saw him outside the door, she turned pale and silent. Shaha explained he had come because he loved her, and he did not understand why she had not answered his letters. And then she began to weep inconsolably. He took her hand, caressed her hair, and felt he had done the right thing coming all the way to Finland, but suddenly she pulled back into the apartment and shut the door behind her. From the other side of the door, Shaha could hear how she wept. He called her name and knocked on the door at regular intervals for many hours. She did not open, not even when she stopped crying.

With the rest of his money, he took a hotel room in the city. He kept returning to her apartment and watching the entrance to the building for hours at a time, which made his body stiff with cold. Now and again he would go down into the buildings basement if the door was open, and there, next to the garbage cans, he collected his strength and the warmth to go out again, once more waiting for her. But she did not come out. And Shaha thought that perhaps she was off visiting family or friends in other cities because of Christmas and New Year's. Finland was an expensive country and his money went quickly. He realized he had to move from the hotel to the hostel in Olympia Stadium. In a few days he would have no money left, neither for food nor a place to live.

"Shaha, why not go back to your own country?" Adán asked, still unable to remember more than the beginning of the long Bangladeshi name and expecting to be corrected now.

But Shaha did not seem to notice the abbreviation of his name at all. And he replied that they loved each other; therefore he would persist until he found her, and then they would get married and live together…in Finland. Because he could not return to Bangladesh after what he had done to his father, a powerful army general, who was now most certainly wounded by and sorely disappointed in the son who had robbed him to leave the country.

For Adán the whole situation was crystal clear. Cautiously he asked Shaha if he had any idea about why she did not want to see him. Shaha thought a long time before he said he did not know. They continued eating.

"And you, Adam, tell me, why are you here in Finland?" Shaha asked straight out.

Adán was convinced that Shaha would not be able to understand his dilemma. Casually he explained that, well, he had always wanted to visit Finland. Now that he lived in Denmark, it was easy to get here. And this was true, but far from the whole truth. Adán found it difficult to read the expression on Shaha's face, but it seemed as if Shaha sensed something missing in the explanation. But no, it would make him sad to talk about Blanca and Bettina. So he shifted his gaze to the large man in a red blazer and blue tie who kept an eye on the customers in the cafeteria. An insignia with gold letters on his coat pocket said "Doorman" in both Swedish and Finnish. A lot of the customers in the cafeteria resembled the seedy residents of Olympia Stadium. Now and then there was a customer about to fall asleep, and before long the doorman shook him with his big hands. And those who sat too long a time in front of an empty cup or bottle were bluntly asked to buy something or clear out.

Everything was different and better in Denmark. Adán finished his coffee and got ready to leave.

"You go now, Adam?" Shaha asked.

"Yes, and you?" It occurred to Adán that Shaha was sorry he was leaving.

Shaha answered, "Too cold outside." Resolution shone in his eyes. "I'll wait here. I have to kill time." And later he would go out to the suburb where "she", the Finnish girl, lived.

Coming out to the street was like rising to the surface from the bottom of a deep sea. Shaha, poor Shaha, who had the strange ability to make him feel better. He began walking aimlessly. He was in Finland after all.

Unlike the area around Olympia Stadium, the city seemed dark and gloomy. Some of the people looked like the elegant Swedes who frequented downtown Copenhagen.

Others reminded him of poverty-stricken Russians he had seen in TV-documentaries. Christmas decorations were still hanging everywhere and contributed a little light to the growing darkness. The cars drove extremely slowly on the snow-covered street, and a closer look revealed a thick glassy layer of ice under the snow. The piercing cold did not worry him. The coat he wore was a present from Bettina on their first Christmas together in Denmark. And the wool sweater Blanca had brought from Chile.

Adán walked up and down the streets trying to escape his thoughts. Blanca or Bettina? His past in Chile or his future in Denmark? Where did he stand? Could love be so contradictory and so cruel? The cold, however, forced him to look for shelter. A modern art museum loomed ahead near the harbor.

It was a small museum, and in one of the few rooms there was an easy chair where he sat down and fell asleep until a uniformed guard shook him by the shoulders and asked him to leave. Out on the empty street, darkness had fallen. The temperature had dropped violently and he began to freeze. Poor Shaha, Adán thought, in his hopeless clothes, with his soft, perhaps aristocratic ways, waiting out in the cold or in the dingy basement for his unattainable Finnish girl. Adán was now hungry as well as cold, but the few open places he saw looked strange and uninviting. The best thing was to go back to Shaha's cafeteria in the main station.

After eating, he got sleepy again. The many days of traveling and the Finnish cold were not to be ignored. But the doorman's sharp eyes kept him from closing his own. He took the notebook from his shoulder bag and after careful deliberation wrote:

El amor está en todas estas extrañas cosas
(Love is in all of these strange things)

que yo hago—para desconocer este doble dolor
(that I do—so as not to know this double pain)

cuando me sueño tu y yo—y tú y yo
(where I dream you and I—and you and I)

An unexpected shadow fell suddenly across his
notebook. He raised his head and there stood Shaha in front
of him with his screaming-red tie. It was hard to see whether
it was a smile or the cold that stretched his lips. Adán quickly
gestured that he sit down.

"I bring you a cup of coffee," Adán said and went to the
counter without waiting for an answer. On the way back with
the steaming cup in his hand, it seemed to him Shaha was
turning his head as one does when trying to read a text that is
upside down. Was it the notebook he was looking at? Adán
smiled to himself. What could a curious Bangladeshi get out
of reading Spanish upside down?

Shaha jerked his head back abruptly when Adán set the
coffee on the table but thanked him and resolutely reached
for his pocket. Adán put a hand on his shoulder and asked
him to be so kind as to accept this cup of coffee as a sign of
friendship. The argument convinced Shaha, who again
thanked him and encircled the hot cup with both of his cold
hands. Adán sat down and closed the notebook. For the time
being there would be no more lines of poetry.

Shaha's sorrowful eyes, which stared at the nothingness
on the surface of the table, spoke of yet another unlucky day.
Finally, he took a cautious sip of hot coffee.

"Adam, what is it you write?" he asked and pointed at
the notebook.

Adán felt a blush of embarrassment on his cheeks.

"Things," he answered. "Different things." No one, not
even Bettina or Blanca, knew about his poetry.

"What kind of things?" Shaha persisted.

Slightly irritated over his own embarrassment, Adán said he was writing a book—a thriller.

"Good..." Shaha suddenly seemed very pensive. Was it perhaps one of those books with an unsolved murder and a detective?

It got worse and worse. Yes, Adán answered, something with detectives and all that. And with a movement that was just as unconscious as it was abrupt, he stuck the notebook back in his shoulder bag. There would be no more talk about his "book."

"I love poems," Shaha said. "Your poet Neruda—he is great!"

Adán nodded. "Yes, he is very great," he said, and got up to go to the toilet.

That evening they got back before opening time at Olympia Stadium. Only two of the Finns from the preceding evening showed up. And there were six new faces that observed the two strange foreigners with undisguised curiosity. The cold and the dark made the wait seem endless. Shaha shook constantly. Worried, Adán offered him his sweater. But, as expected, the offer was refused.

Later Adán took a shower. As soon as the warm water began to cascade down, the usual images assaulted him. Bettina, who had welcomed him to Grøfthøj Park, helped him recover from the torture, and offered him a life in the foreign country Denmark once was. And then Blanca, the girl from his neighborhood in Temuco, the first one he had ever been with and who stood in the street crying when the soldiers hauled him off. An evil fate forced him to make a choice, and he would lose, no matter what.

When he lay in bed reading the last lines he had written, Shaha went gliding by with his delicate movements on the way to the shower. A few minutes later he came out again dressed in silky pajamas and a net over his hair! He walked over to Adán's bed and stopped in front of him.

He said, "Adam, while I was under the shower, I was thinking very much of you." He sat on the bed at Adán's feet. Adán hopped back a few centimeters in his bed. Ignoring his reaction, Shaha laid a hand on the bed, touching one of his feet, which fortunately, Adán thought in a fleeting second, was covered by the blanket. Shaha overstepped excessively the precepts of how and where men talked with each other. But, well, Shaha was not from Chile—he was from another planet. Shaha said he would never forget the cup of coffee Adán, his friend in Finland, had bought him in the cafeteria at the railway station. Then, he got up from the bed and went over to his own. His strange perfume was still hanging in the air. Shaha never ceased to astonish him.

This comic moment was quickly replaced by the usual thoughts that forced Adán's mind to shuttle endlessly and painfully back and forth between Blanca and Bettina. Tired of being so miserable, he sighed and tried to write a few lines in his notebook, but without success.

He looked around, trying to gather his thoughts, and suddenly met Shaha's eyes. They were the only ones awake. Adán smiled and waved like one does to someone who is very far away, and Shaha waved back in the same manner.

Again they sat across from each other in the cafeteria at the railway station. The huge man with the "Doorman" insignia on his jacket pocket gave them a friendly nod of recognition. "Good morning," Shaha said in response in a calm, charitable tone, which made Adán imagine Shaha in Bangladesh, surrounded by servants in his rich father's house.

While they were having their breakfast, they were accosted by a woman who waved a camera and with gesticulations asked permission to photograph them. They agreed. Afterward, she asked the doorman to take a picture of her with them. They did not feel at all disturbed or embarrassed, and when she left they continued with their breakfast, as before. Shaha munched his French fries with ketchup and drank hot chocolate. Adán had bought a larger combo than the day before. Finland's cold required a lot more calories than the Danish winter did. It was a mystery to him how Shaha, all skin and bones, could survive in such clothes and with hardly anything at all to eat. Adán knew very well it was useless, but tried anyway, to talk some sense into him.

"Shaha, what if she don't want to see you again?"

Shaha looked as if he were putting things together in his head. And Adán hoped he was beginning to see the light. For if he did not, his blind love would end up killing him, helped by hunger and the Finnish cold.

But Shaha was unshakable—of course she would see him again at some point or other…because they loved each other. After all, they were together once—the night before she left Bangladesh, and you only did something like that if you loved someone with all your heart. Perhaps this was the very day he would be lucky. And then she would understand his love and agree to his plans for the future.

Poor Shaha, hopelessly in love, had the strange ability to make him feel less unlucky.

"How is your detective book, Adam?" Shaha asked.

"My detective book? " Then Adán remembered the day before when his poems had become a crime novel. Now, with the notebook safely tucked in the shoulder bag, he found it easier, even fun, to talk about his detective novel. Well, he wrote now and then, as inspiration struck him.

Shaha asked whether he could tell him a little bit about the plot. And Adán explained it was about a detective who was trying to solve a murder with two women suspects; both of them were very beautiful, and they both loved the detective…but he had to do his job and point out the one who was guilty. A complicated case because along the way the detective had fallen in love with both of them.

Shaha seemed very interested. But Adán, who thought the story was getting out of hand, changed the subject.

They had been sitting there for a long time without

buying anything. But the doorman kept on smiling amicably at their table. It was clear they could stay there as long as they liked without ordering anything else. Still, Adán thought it was time to stretch his legs.

In contrast to the day before, when he had rambled around in the center of Helsinki, this time he walked in a nearly straight line as long as possible. And step after step in the snow, with the cold glued to his face, he walked along towards nowhere. Maybe the empty space of fatigue would give him the answer he needed. What should he do when he got back to Grøfthøj Park? But the more he walked, the less tired he became. Suddenly he was on his back on the snow and the ice beneath it. With great difficulty, he sat up and realized he felt pain in his right shoulder, and that it had gotten dark. An old woman came out of a house. She spoke Finnish and tried to help him up. It wasn't necessary; he could get up himself easily. But she took his hand and brought him into her house. At first he didn't want to follow her, but she insisted, nearly dragging him in. She talked incessantly and sat him in a chair, brought him a cup of hot chocolate, which he drank while he listened without understanding a word. He felt very comfortable in the curious little home where all of mysterious Finland bade him welcome. They smiled at one another. The old lady spoke and Adán nodded. Afterwards he bowed many times, saying, "Thank you, thank you" in Danish, which the lady clearly understood. He shook her hand while she kept on talking, and he still did not understand a word. Finally he was out in the dark and the snow again.

The best thing was to head back to Helsinki, to Shaha's cafeteria at the railway station. Strange, aside from the old lady, he had seen hardly anyone on the streets. Nor did many of the windows in the houses show any sign of activity even though it was only a few hours til New Year's Eve. The dark prevented him from reconstructing the exact way back, but the light from the center of Helsinki could be seen farther out in the night, and he set off in that direction.

The cold had nearly paralyzed his facial muscles. And when he began to eat, it took a few minutes before his jawbone could find the right movements. After eating, he drank a lot of coffee. The warmth rose again in his body, making him sleepy. But the new doorman let him understand that there were eyes watching him. Where was Shaha? Maybe everything had been just a misunderstanding, and Shaha was enjoying the company of his dream girl in a warm apartment. Yes, he had to admit it—he missed Shaha…with his screaming-red tie and his annoying questions about Neruda. He missed the happy days in Chile before he became politically active when New Year's Eve was a joy that made people embrace and wish each other the best for the New Year. He missed Denmark, too, the country where he knew everything, the country without doormen to keep an eye on his fatigue, the country that was now his home. He missed Blanca. And he missed Bettina, too. He missed them and their love and the few, happy moments when he had loved one of them without thinking of the other. Shit! How depressed he was—he did not even have any desire to continue his poem.

He reached Olympia Stadium a little past 8:00 P.M., paid the usual fee to the attendant, and went into the sleeping area. And it was a real joy to see Shaha again. On the other hand, it would have been better if Shaha were with his Finnish girl now and didn't have to sleep another night in the hostel. Aside from the attendant, they were the only ones in Olympia Stadium. Even the Helsinki bums could find a better place to spend New Year's Eve. Shaha sat at the only table, where the noisy Finns used to gather. He had just taken a shower and was dressed in his glamorous pajamas, the faithful net over his head and smelling of his odd perfume.

"I'm happy to see you, Adam. I was afraid you wouldn't come tonight," said Shaha.

It was only now Adán realized how defeated Shaha looked. Adán said in a cheerful tone that the feeling was mutual. Shaha smiled faintly and looked at his hands, which rested tired and dispirited on the table. Perhaps he was finally beginning to perceive the hell his love was leading him to. Good for him, thought Adán, as he got ready to take his daily hot shower—the sooner he wakes up to reality the better.

After his shower, Adán dressed and sat at the table. He was in the right mood for a few lines, and he took out his notebook. Shaha sat so still and quiet that his presence was not disturbing. After a while he wrote:

El amor no desea para nadie lo mejor
(Love doesn't desire the best for anyone)

porque el amor sólo desea la perfección
(for love has only one desire—perfection)

Adán looked up at the ceiling to find more words for his feelings. And Shaha said, as if he leaped out of his own world, "I like very much Neruda's *Twenty Love Poems and a Song of Despair.* You know that book, Adam?"

There was Shaha and his Neruda again. But this time he was not irritated. He wanted to help Shaha bear his burden. In school he had read a couple of poems from that book. He did not remember any of it today. But Shaha had withdrawn into himself again—his eyes stared toward everything and nothing. Adán concentrated on his poem. After a long while he wrote:

El amor no puede ser la felicidad de nadie
(Love can't be anyone's happiness)

Porque el amor solo busca lo imposible
(because love seeks only the impossible)

Adán pushed the notebook away. The movement brought
Shaha back into the world of the living. He turned his head a
little, probably to decipher the text, which from his angle
was upside down. Adán smiled, pleased at his curiosity.

"Your detective is okay?" asked Shaha.

"Yes. He is okay," Adán answered.

"He found out which woman is the bad one?"

"Not yet, Shaha. Not yet."

Suddenly the attendant appeared. He said that probably
no more people would show up at this point, so few minutes
before the New Year. Was it okay if he slipped away to see
his family? Both of them answered, as one, it was okay. He
did not live far from the stadium and he would be back
sometime during the night. In the unlikely event that some
guests showed up, well, they could just have a bed. Was that
okay? And again they answered that it was.

The attendant hurried off. And the Indian from Temuco
and the Bangladeshi from Dacca were the only people in the
huge white building in the middle of a field, which was called
Olympia Stadium. They sat across from each other, silent
and thoughtful, as the minutes pulled them both into 1977.

Suddenly they realized it was past midnight. They stood up
and shook hands.

"Happy New Year, Adam."

"Happy New Year, Shaha."

Adán really felt like embracing Shaha, clapping him on
the shoulders, and wishing him the best for the New Year as
he would have done with a Chilean. But, shit! How could
you embrace a man in silky pajamas, a net over his head, and
surrounded by perfume? He settled for pressing his hand
harder and saying, "I'm very happy you are here, Shaha."

"You are a good friend, Adam."

Adán went over to his bag and took out a chocolate bar. He divided it in half, gave a piece to Shaha and lifted his piece like one does with a glass to say cheers.

"Happy New Year," he said. And Shaha answered in the same manner. Then they each bit a piece of their chocolate.

Adán woke in the middle of the night. His watch read 5:30. Shaha was sleeping. They were the only ones still in the sleeping area. Had the attendant returned from the bosom of his family? He turned around in bed and came to the conclusion that he would not fall asleep again. What was Blanca doing now...? Maybe she was with the group of Chileans who celebrated New Year's in the recreation room of one of the concrete buildings. And Bettina...? She was most likely alone. She avoided people when she was feeling bad. It was good that he was here. But how many more days would he stay at Olympia Stadium?

Adán got up slowly and began to put on his clothes. Finland, this charitable no-man's-land had spared him a New Year's Eve in Grøfthøj Park. But Finland would not give him the answer to how to handle his dilemma. He had to go back to Denmark. Now.

Carefully, nearly soundlessly, he gathered up his things. He gave Shaha a last glance and walked down the long corridor that led to the entrance. In the grimy office, the attendant slept in an armchair.

Adán came out into the white landscape. Since the distance from the stadium to the main station was manageable and no trolleys were running at this time of day, he intended to walk. He was sorry about not saying goodbye to Shaha. But saying goodbye to people he liked was not his strong suit.

What a strange land, Finland...and he remembered the face of the sweet old lady who tried to help him up after his fall on the snow, who hosted him in her little wooden house, and spoke kind, incomprehensible words to him. Strange land…it still seemed unpopulated and deserted. And there was something so moving about this never-ending snow. Again he had the urge to shout something or other, to make himself felt in this overwhelming landscape. But he was not the one who shouted. No, it was Shaha! He stood at the entrance to Olympia Stadium and waved and called to him.

That was the last thing Adán had expected. Well…but now there was no other choice than to say the goodbye he had tried to avoid. Shaha was a continual surprise. Adán went back to the entrance of the stadium.

"You leave now?" Shaha seemed sad about it.

Adán, already embarrassed about his attempt at flight, explained that he had to go back to Denmark…now.

"Adam, there is something I want to tell you," Shaha said, and it sounded important.

Adán waited with a certain suspense.

"Do you remember the first time we met, at your bed?"

Adán thought about it…and he remembered when Shaha wanted to take his bed even though it was obviously occupied. Now what?

Shaha said he was sorry, very sorry. He had not intended to take his bed. He was reading his poem.

"Reading my poem?"

Yes. The open notebook lying on the bed had caught Shaha's attention when he came into the sleeping area from the hallway. A single glance was enough to see that the writing in the notebook was a poem, with a few lines on a whole page. And a poem was not one of the first things he expected to see on his arrival at Olympia Stadium. And Shaha, the student of literature who loved poems, could not resist the temptation to look at the notebook. He was greatly surprised when he saw it was written in Spanish—Neruda's language.

"Do you understand Spanish, Shaha?!" Adán looked him in the eyes.

"I'm very sorry, Adam," Shaha said and explained. After reading *Twenty Poems of Love and a Song of Despair*, he wanted to learn Spanish, even if just a little. His father agreed to get him private Spanish lessons. A woman from the Spanish Embassy came two days a week and tutored Shaha in Neruda's language.

Adán blushed. And Shaha said he had intended just to take a quick peek at the text in the notebook. But the word *amor* that he knew all too well ran through the text…so he ignored the noisy Finns, forgot himself a moment, and kept on reading the two open pages—until Adán came out of the shower room.

Adán shook his head, embarrassed. His hardboiled detective book had been revealed as a love poem.

"Es una linda poema," (It's a beautiful poem), Shaha said with a funny accent and the classic mistake of foreigners: Not all words that end with an a are feminine. "It's much better than a detective book, Adam."

Adán asked why he had not said anything about it. Shaha was shivering already and rubbed his hands. Even though they stood in the entryway to the stadium, the thin pajamas and the hairnet gave no protection against the cold that forced itself in. Shaha answered that one did not read other people's love poems, because no one writes that kind of poem without a reason. He was afraid of Adán's reaction if he admitted reading two pages in the notebook.

"You are not angry, Adam?"

"No, Shaha, I'm not angry."

They looked away from each other, each toward an indefinite point in the cold, white distance. Silence hastened the farewell. Once more Adán felt the urge to embrace him, to clap him on the back with both hands, and wish him luck and happiness. But once again—how could you embrace a perfumed man in silky pajamas with a hairnet over his head?

Adán settled for putting out his hand and saying, "I hope you will find your Finnish girl, Shaha."

"I will find her, Adam. Because I love her."

And now Adán gripped Shaha's hand with both of his. "I wish you very much luck, Shaha." And then he turned and walked fast in the direction of the road.

"Adam!" Shaha called. Adán stopped and turned around. Shaha was waving with his whole arm. "Good luck for you too, Adam!" and then he disappeared into Olympia Stadium, back to the Finland that Adán was about to leave.

Adán kept standing in the middle of the path and his own inner void. After a few minutes he walked slowly back to the stadium entrance. Inside, he continued toward the attendant's office. He knocked on the window, woke the man, wished him a Happy New Year, and asked him for a favor. The man answered sleepily but kindly that thanks to Adán and Shaha he had slipped home to his family during the night. So Adán took his notebook and a ballpoint pen out of his shoulder bag. He wrote on the cover of the notebook: Para Shaha, mi amigo, en estos extraños días finlandeses (To Shaha, my friend, in these strange Finnish days). Adam. That he would end up giving his love poems to a man…Adán smiled incredulously at himself. Afterwards he asked the attendant, "Please, later, could you give this to my friend?"

"To the strange man from Bangladesh?"

"Yes," Adán said, "This is for him."

"Of course," the man said, took the notebook, and laid it on his desk. "He will get it," he assured him.

On the way to Helsinki, he stopped and looked back for the last time. In the distance, Olympia Stadium rested in its own unshakable grandeur. And his thoughts returned to poor Shaha—a prisoner of a love as enormous and unshakable as Olympia Stadium, the place where he lived. As for himself— well, at this moment it occurred to him just as clearly as unavoidably that no matter what he did, he would lose, lose a part of himself, too. He had known that already. But this time he accepted it. He would not choose between Blanca and Bettina because he could not. Instead he would let circumstances choose for him. Sooner or later, Blanca or Bettina or both of them, would leave him. And a pain, a pain he feared, waited for him ahead. But he was ready to accept it. And should it become unbearable...well, then, he would write poems until the storm was over.

Adán continued toward Helsinki. A two, maybe three days' journey lay between him and his home in Denmark.

The Return of Roy Jackson

Even at an early age, when he was only a nine-year-old Colombian boy, Artemio Sandoval decided that when he grew up he would be a writer.

The child Artemio had just written another story about Roy Jackson: his own fictitious cowboy who rode through wild landscapes while he shot at Indians and bandits. In "The Return of Roy Jackson," as the story was called, the hero, after many years' absence, had returned to his home town and freed it from the iron grip of a tyrannical villain.

The child used to end all his stories with a drawing, and full of excitement, he concentrated on making the very first stroke: a light, horizontal line drew Roy Jackson's jawbone, and from there he assumed his full shape gradually. In this scene the hero would stand in the main street with a smoking pistol in his right hand and a foot on the evil villain, who would lie lifeless with a quite visible bullet hole in his forehead.

Suddenly the child's mother came in, and her usual flurry seemed to fill the whole room in a flash. It was the flurry that kept the family together in spite of the eternally threatening poverty. She stopped and smiled; her youngest child was far off in his own world when he was bent over a piece of paper with pencil in hand. She went over to him and hugged him, closed her eyes and stared into the future. Perhaps some far-off day everything would be different and better, probably not for her, but for her children. "Some day you will be a famous author, my Temito," she said in a dreamy sort of voice and hugged her child tighter. Temito was the mother's loving way of saying my beloved little Artemio. "Mother is so proud of you," she added. Then she kissed him on the forehead and left the room.

The child continued drawing until the picture was finished. And it was only when he had written THE END at the bottom of the page, right under Roy Jackson, that he once again noticed the sultry heat of the Colombian night. As was his habit, he took off his shirt and lay face down flat on the floor to cool his body against the cool tiles. He felt his heart pounding with joy. A new Roy Jackson story was finished, and his mother had been proud of him. And suddenly he saw himself as a grown man, happy, proud, and writing one book after the other while thousands of people read every line and every word. And now he knew what he would be when he grew up.

But there was something the child Artemio could not know. He could not possibly know that forty years later in a distant country, Denmark, he would remember the hot night when he convinced himself he would be a writer.

When Artemio Sandoval became a young man, he chose not to build a future by going to the university, but by dedicating himself to activities he wholeheartedly believed would bring justice to the poor of Colombia.

But in 1969, the 25-year-old Artemio Sandoval was forced to flee Colombia. In 1972 after a chaotic knocking about through a number of Latin American countries, he crossed the strip of desert that marks the border between Peru and Chile and headed south. His encounter with Santiago fascinated him. The cool climate and the nearly organized tempo of the city stood in sharp contrast to everything he had experienced in Latin America. He settled down in Santiago.

In the period between 1970 and 1973, under President Salvador Allende's regime, Chile became a refuge for left-wing exiles from all over Latin America. The Chileans had always been extremely proud of the stanza in their national anthem that says that the oppressed from all countries can find asylum in Chile ("o el asilo contra la opresión"). But when the right-wing military coup occurred in September 1973, the new leaders ignored this most beautiful stanza. And an unknown number of refugees were mistreated and/or killed in the country that once had accepted them with open arms.

Artemio Sandoval realized that he had to say goodbye to Santiago, the city where he had finally managed to settle down. He spent three months in a refugee camp for foreigners on the outskirts of Santiago before he arrived in Copenhagen one cold January night in 1974. He was thirty years old.

Copenhagen was a true enchantment. What a city—with lakes, bicycle paths, well-regulated traffic, and courteous people. Compared to Copenhagen, Santiago was just as Latin American as Bogotá or Quito.

As soon as he found a place to live, a residence hall, he opened the black plastic bag he had carried with him since his flight from Colombia.

Notes, a number of stories, and a novel. It was the priceless treasure the black bag had carried from country to country. Artemio Sandoval took everything out and laid it in a pile on the desk. And then he smiled, remembering himself hiding in an apartment in Caracas, along Colombia's dangerous roads, in the jungles of Ecuador, in the worst slums of Lima, in Santiago's cafés, and later in the UN refugee camp. Each time circumstances had provided him with a little time, a modicum of peace, he had written. The stack of papers on his desk was proof of his strength and unquenchable will to live.

But the stack of papers was also proof of a long and changeable road covered with wrecked political dreams and frustrated authorial ambitions. Neither the short stories nor the novel were completed, for his life had unfolded itself in violent stops and starts, from day to day, from place to place. People, cities, whole countries had appeared and disappeared the same way that a passenger in a train experiences the world on the other side of the window.

He spread the material out across the desk carefully and

started reading at random the scraps of paper, loose pages, and notebooks. Certain passages gripped him strongly. And some downright genial sentences made him read out loud and get up and walk back and forth in the few square meters of his room.

At one point he went over to the room's only window. And the full moon, which made the world outside visible, took him by surprise. Obviously many hours had gone by since he had opened the black bag. The light of the full moon bathed the residence hall on the other side of the lawn and the parking lot with its cars and bicycles…everything was covered or dappled with snow, and not a single movement, not a single living being disturbed the peace that covered this both strange and fascinating Danish landscape. He could not remember ever enjoying the privilege of observing such a consummate peacefulness.

Artemio Sandoval closed his eyes, breathed deeply, and held in the air as long as he could. Then he exhaled slowly and opened his eyes. Nothing had changed outside. Everything was still there, just as serene as before, as if this Danish landscape wanted to hug him and make him a part of it. He smiled again. From now on, nothing could keep him from becoming a writer.

Day was breaking slowly but steadily when he closed the curtains and lay down to sleep.

In the course of the following months, Artemio Sandoval was busy trying to find the answer to the following question: which of his writings should he choose to finish first?

The countless notes offered good linguistic wording and ideas for stories and novels, but they were an impenetrable jungle and so could not serve as a foundation for a budding authorship.

It was another case with the short stories. There was a total of eleven. They were literary experiments attesting to his creative talent. For example, one story took place in the head of a person about to attempt something dangerous and magnificent. One train of thought succeeded the other in a kind of inner monolog which was only interrupted by sounds and voices coming from outside. What a unique short story collection it could be!

Then there was the novel, *The Labyrinth*—he had written about 150 pages of that—a powerful social-realistic description where people help and hinder each other in the search for meaning in life. But only one of them attains this meaning. The story was constructed of fragments consisting of a single sentence or of many pages. In truth a trailblazing novel.

Being able to choose between different possibilities is usually seen as a propitious, if not fortunate, situation. But for Artemio Sandoval, the short story collection and the novel became the source of unexpected distress.

Every time he committed himself to one of the possibilities and began to write, he had a feeling of terrible loss. To work on only one wonderful book meant to give up on another just as wonderful book. He was really aware that this train of thought was a complete absurdity. And yet weeks and months went by without his being able to get started.

Nothing was more important to him than becoming a writer, a well-known writer. But as soon as he sat down and started to write, he got restless and could not concentrate, as if his limbs were chained to horses, each pulling in its own direction.

One evening more than a year after he had opened the black bag, and during a thoughtful walk along Copenhagen's lakes, he suddenly hit upon the root of his distress.

He had long been accustomed to working on as many as three writing projects in a single day. In the morning, sitting in a battered bus, he would tackle a new story. And on the same day in the evening at some cheap country pension or other, he would begin writing something completely different. He was quite simply not used to thinking about a single story over a longer period of time.

For almost a year he had been paralyzed. That he had not been able to see such a trifle—inconceivable! And here he discovered the wisdom in the Danish proverb that went something like not being able to see the forest for the trees. Clearly, the urge to write a book had kept him from seeing precisely what kept him from getting started.

He hurried home. Before he opened the door to his room he saw his future book before him—a collection of experimental stories that would carve his name into the world of literature forever. Yes, a long walk along the lakes could work miracles. How lucky to live in Copenhagen, a city with lakes in its center.

At once he felt relieved, skillful again...possessed of a future full of accomplishment. In one year, or more precisely, in July 1976, his wonderful short-story collection would be mailed to a Spanish publisher.

But July 1976 came, and not a single one of the eleven stories was yet completed. The cause of this catastrophe became quickly apparent—he had used too much time for everything else but writing—such as finding a powerful, stimulating title for the book that would serve as a thematic thread though all the stories. Nor had it been easy to compose the query letter to inform the publishers on how the work should be read. His material was spread out over so many different kinds of paper that it had to be retyped. And finally, the choice of the story that should begin the collection had, in spite of all his new awareness, turned out to be surprisingly difficult.

Artemio Sandoval had to surrender to one inexorable fact—writing a book definitely demanded much more than he had imagined. One could well believe that this recognition would destroy his courage. But, no, on the contrary. He felt important, as if accomplishing a unique mission. Books would be his contribution to the world. And for the first time in his poverty-stricken and peripatetic life, he experienced the self-worth that knowledge of one's own role in life provides.

It was from this moment that he really began to resemble an established writer. His clothes, movements, voice—his whole being took on a kind of literary appearance. Little by little people in his circle of acquaintances referred to him with a certain respect as "the author" or "the one who writes."

Endowed with these new experiences of the demanding life of a writer, Artemio Sandoval revised his work habits. Deadlines were a bad thing. He would write freely, out of inspiration and desire, without thinking about whether the work should be finished in a month or in a hundred years.

After careful consideration, he chose "The Voice that Fell Silent" as the story in the collection he should finish first. And to avoid distraction, he locked all the other stories in a cabinet. This story consisted mainly of a conversation among a number of voices going on while a murder in their midst was slowly revealed. As the title clearly indicated, one of the voices fell silent, leading the reader to the identity of the murderer. A demanding task. The *niveau* for this literary work should be established right from the beginning.

But an unexpected phenomenon ruined his plans and visions. It was as if he did not know what to do with the plot's mounting suspense. Both language and inspiration failed him and went flat in an inexplicable way. How frustrating; he had finally developed the discipline needed to concentrate on a single literary project...and he still could not get on with it. He came to a complete stop.

It was 1978. Artemio Sandoval was getting desperate when, during yet another anxious walk along the lakes, he recovered his confidence in himself and his future as an author once more. It happened when he stopped and let his eyes casually roam along the lake until he spotted a bird floating carefree on the quiet water. He could not determine what kind of a bird it was because suddenly it lifted from the water and flew toward a diminutive spot of earth, a toy island in the middle of the lake. He had never known very much about birds, but wasn't it some kind of duck or gull, the birds most often seen in Denmark? The bird flew over the toy island and continued in the direction of Sweden until it disappeared into the distance. The uncomplicated naturalness the bird showed when it rose and flew away from everything touched him. And it forced him to reflect on his own complicated and unnatural situation—possessed by a burning desire to write but not able to do it. He was a bird that could not rise and fly!

And he realized that something like that—being blocked in the middle of a creative process—had happened to all great artists throughout history. Moreover, in his original plan, nothing should be forced by haste or deadlines. So why was he fighting an obstinate battle to finish *The Voice That Fell Silent*? It was never his intention that his writing should become an inner war.

Maybe it was a good idea to take a break. If he let time work by itself, if he let it calmly bring inspiration and creativity back to him, then he sooner or later would certainly rise and fly like a bird.

And time passed until an apparently innocent episode made Artemio Sandoval think about it: namely, that time passed. It happened during a gathering of Danes and Latin Americans who were enjoying wine, dancing, and the topics of conversation the mixed company usually occasioned.

Artemio Sandoval was hurrying to the toilet when a young Danish girl came up to him."

"Hey, I want to talk with you!"

Like most Latin Americans, Artemio Sandoval had a weakness for blond hair and blue eyes. Pleasantly astounded, he said:

"And why is that?"

"I want to read your books." She shrugged her shoulders apologetically. "But I don't know what they're called. I'd like to take them out of the library."

At first he lit up. This young Danish girl approached him, the author. But a second later he was seized by an anxiety he had not imagined could exist. What was he to say to the girl?! The painful silence between him and this unexpected beauty forced him to stammer out the truth. Well, yes, he was just working on a book, yes, on several books that would soon be finished as soon as he pulled himself together, and so on.

The girl's polite disappointment crushed him. He had clearly robbed her of the happiness of meeting a real author.

That night Artemio Sandoval could not sleep. All the extra attention he had often enjoyed because he was an author! And then there were the women, who, now that he looked back on it, had obviously felt attracted to him because he was a writer. But where could one read his books? How embarrassing!

The following days were no better. Simple arithmetic nearly made him panic. He had come to Denmark in 1974. And now it was 1983. A whole nine years—and a neglected authorship was still awaiting him.

Naturally he had thought now and then about how time was passing—but at those times he had felt that there was still plenty of time to write one or more books.

From one day to the next, Artemio Sandoval could not recognize himself. Suddenly he stood there, caught between the time already wasted and the time he was about to waste. And life itself ran from him like water between his fingers.

Again the lakes of Copenhagen saw the desolated Artemio Sandoval wander along their banks seeking the key to the authorship that would justify his existence.

At the age of 38 he could not think of becoming a mechanic or a doctor. For him there was only one way. With all his talent and burning love for literature, why could he not finish a book?

Desperate, he examined himself and his career as an author. Somewhere or other there has to be a trail, a sign. His doggedness paid off and the answer hit him harder than a clenched fist.

He did not write with one ending in mind, but with various, shifting endings. How simple…! In "The Voice that Fell Silent," for example, a person would fall silent and reveal himself as the murderer—but which of the increasing number of people and voices? He still did not know. At least once a week he changed the murderer. At one point he had even operated with two murderers and two voices that would fall silent, which contradicted the title, formulated as it was in the singular.

But there was a problem, a big problem. His desire and energy to write sprang out of the very freedom of writing without an ending in sight. His pleasure came from daring experiments, sophisticated formulations, surprising turns of plot, and so on. He wrote to write…not to conclude! And that was fine. But it would never make him a famous author.

An overwhelming sense of powerlessness overtook Artemio Sandoval. For it was in 1975 that he discovered the necessity of focusing on just one literary project. But it was only now that his incapacity to write his way to an ending was clear to him. Was he so stupid that he could only realize one thing at a time—one, and that during an interval of nearly 10 years? It was hard to imagine. On the whole, it was hard to be a human being, Artemio Sandoval thought.

Gone were those happy moments where he could fly freely, lost in the landscapes and human relationships created in his fantasy. Now he was a prisoner of the obligation to a single story and its conclusion.

This loss slowly changed his feelings toward the art he had lived for. Literature changed into a crude distortion of reality. For nothing in the universe could be squeezed between a beginning and an ending. Why on earth should a story be presented from a beginning to an end? A story, any story at all, was in principle endless!

There followed a period of several months where Artemio Sandoval underwent a striking change. Those around him observed that he spoke disparagingly of literature as an art, and of authors as human beings. And if his assertions were not followed up, he simply forced the conversation in that direction. An inner rage poured out of him.

What an absurd world! The alliance between authors and publishers hawked the illusion of the demarcated story to millions of readers who threw themselves into the first page simply to get to the last. The readers, these bewildered fools, bought a beginning and an ending—something that could only exist on printed paper and in their heads.

That his listeners sometimes nodded receptively at these effusions encouraged him to continue unrestrained. How could you call…something that moved from point A to point B in a predictable pattern…literary art? Art and artifice… was there any difference at all?

In ancient days there were myths—living, free, and endless myths that were always enriched with new actors and developed in just as many directions as there were storytellers to tell them. Modern man had created this fundamental deceit called the well-rounded story. And so on.

At last Artemio Sandoval saw himself: a Colombian Don Quijote fighting windmills, in Denmark. He was tired of being angry. Really tired of not being a writer. It was decidedly easier to see oneself under fatigue than under anger, he discovered. And he resigned himself to the fact that one could not write a never-ending story, much less send it to a publisher. Like all other books, his would have to have a beginning and an end.

One could claim with some justice that this crisis, triggered by a completely innocent Danish girl, put Artemio Sandoval on the track he had been seeking for years. And little by little, in the same way his story began to take shape after its ending, he adjusted his days to the work of writing.

He sorted out his friends and acquaintances, including girlfriends, according to their contribution to his inspiration or ideas. He only bought and listened to music that induced the right mood. Television he reduced to a few comprehensive news programs. He even carefully administrated where and when he drank coffee during the day. Writing became the guide to his existence.

And it was hard. There were moments when he really wanted to give up and forget about it all. But, no, he had to continue now and struggle to become the only thing he possibly could become at his age. It was a battle between the pipe-dream writer and the real writer. And he had to win this battle, whatever the cost.

And then, one happy day at the end of 1991, nearly five years after the Danish girl asked her stinging question, Artemio Sandoval finished his novel, The Labyrinth. Before thinking too much about it, he made five copies and sent them to five different Spanish publishers.

From that day forward, the postman and the letter slot's daily snap became an obsession—a disappointing obsession because days and weeks went by without a single letter from Spain.

After seven months he could not endure the wait any longer, and with his heart in his mouth, he picked up the telephone and began to dial the country code of Spain.

At the first two publishers, they remembered the book but had not read it yet...and they probably would not, either; from now on they intended to concentrate on young Spanish authors. The third publisher had gone bankrupt a few months earlier. And the fourth said, without giving any reason, that the book was not of interest to them.

A stunned Artemio Sandoval realized that telephoning had brought him nothing but misery. Nevertheless he dialed the number of the fifth publisher. It could not get any worse, anyway.

A Spaniard, a man, answered the phone at the other end, and introduced himself. Likewise, Artemio Sandoval introduced himself.

"Oh…you're the one who lives in Denmark, the author of *The Labyrinth,*" the Spaniard said, sounding really receptive. "It's one of the most exciting pieces of experimental literature I've read. I mean that, really."

"Thank you," Artemio Sandoval said, while he thought… at last!

They exchanged a few polite formalities. The Spaniard seemed eager to know various things about Denmark, and Artemio Sandoval answered, tense with impatience to get down to business. Suddenly, in a way that seemed to him completely out of context, he heard the Spaniard say, "…and that's why, unfortunately, we can't publish your book."

"But, you just said that it was one of the most exciting books you've read," he pulled himself together enough to reply.

"Yes. And I really mean it," said the Spaniard sincerely. "But, look, you live in Denmark, and that's real problematical."

"Could you…could you please explain that a little more?"

"Of course. It isn't convincing having a Latin American author who writes in a country with civilized inhabitants, snow, and a royal family. Do you follow me?"

Artemio Sandoval thought he had gone crazy and was hallucinating. In a barely controlled voice, he named a number of famous Latin American authors who lived in Spain, France, and Italy. But the Spaniard continued, unmoved—those writers were already famous when they moved to Europe. Readers wanted the real thing—a Latin American who wrote surrounded by oppression, corruption, poverty, and scorching heat, where families lived packed together under wretched circumstances, promiscuous relationships, where the brother went to work on the sister as soon as the parents fell asleep... "Do you follow me now?" the Spaniard said after his long stream of arguments.

The rest of the conversation was like being tossed down a dark hole. And the fall did not stop when he hung up the phone. The following months he could neither eat nor sleep properly and seemed a ghost with a distant look and hopeless gait.

Darkness fell with all of its weight on Artemio Sandoval. Life refused to give him the role he had always dreamed of.

It was in this alarming condition that one sunny day while walking along the Langelinje, he caught sight of a Catholic priest sitting on a bench, gazing out to sea. The priest was an old man, dark-skinned, and looked neither European nor Asian. He could only be Latin American.

Artemio Sandoval wondered what a Catholic priest dressed in classic cassock was doing there, near the Little Mermaid, in one of the most Danish landscapes anywhere. Before he managed to speculate on an explanation, he suddenly recalled his own Catholic childhood and the intense devout moments in front of the wooden altar of his local church. And he also remembered the human decency the people of the church exhibited in a world characterized by callousness and chaos. Touched by these childhood memories and by the need to emerge from the tunnel that kept him from living life, he went over to the priest and said in Spanish, "Padre, may I speak with you?"

The priest turned his eyes from the sea toward him. As expected, he answered in Latin American Spanish. "You're doing that already, my son."

"I'm feeling miserable," Artemio Sandoval said straight out. His childhood memories made him feel he had known the priest a long time, which in a way was true. "I can't get on with my life," he added and felt better already.

The priest scrutinized him a minute with his calm eyes and asked if he were a Chilean refugee. Artemio Sandoval declared he was a refugee all right, but from Colombia. His accent was Chilean because he had lived in Chile, and now he was living in Denmark and socialized with Chilean refugees.

"And here you can't get on with your life?" the priest asked.

"I just can't become what I want to become. You see, Padre...I want to..."

The priest sighed deeply and looked out toward the sea. Was he irritated all of a sudden?

"I hope I'm not disturbing you," Artemio Sandoval said, hesitantly.

"You're both disturbing and irritating me, my son," the priest said as he turned toward him again. "You have obviously forgotten how life is in Latin America. It's a serious sin in God's eyes not to be able to get on with your life when you are living securely and comfortably here in Denmark."

Artemio Sandoval bowed his head. After a pause, he said, "You're right, Padre. I'm ashamed."

They fell silent, and Artemio Sandoval did indeed feel ashamed. Unexpectedly the priest asked if he could under-stand English and knew John Wayne.

Artemio Sandoval's sense of shame was replaced by puzzlement. Only the priest's dignified bearing kept his expectations high, and he answered in the affirmative.

Satisfied, the priest nodded and said, "Listen, I don't have much time for you. People in your situation need precise and, above all, short truths." He lifted his voice. "My son, listen to what I want to tell you."

"I'm listening, Padre."

"And remember, this isn't the word of God. And it isn't mine, either. These are John Wayne's words."

"I'm listening, Padre." Artemio Sandoval shut his eyes.

The priest said, "A man got to do what a man got to do."

In spite of the priest's horrible pronunciation, Artemio Sandoval understood the words very well and their meaning in Spanish. With his eyes still closed, he repeated every word: Un hombre tiene que hacer lo que un hombre tiene que hacer. It was as if the message emptied his head of thoughts and centered him in himself again. And he immediately noticed how his heart beat and the blood coursed within him. The message spoke an incontrovertible language—he was a man with duties here in life! He had grown up with this essential knowledge, but it had been buried under the treadmill of doubt and despondency he had wandered into. He shook his head.

"I have been stupid, Padre," he said.

"Say no more, and go on your way now, my son. You got things to do."

"Thank you, Padre. Goodbye."

And the old priest went back to looking at the sea.

Artemio Sandoval hurried home. The ecclesiastical slap on the wrist had really worked. Yes, a real man becomes stronger under pressure, gets up from the floor, fulfills his duty, fights for his life. Shit! The comfortable years in Denmark had made him forget the good old precepts.

But here was the same Artemio Sandoval, who had fought for Colombia's poor, who had survived highway robbers in Venezuela and an assault in the slums of Lima... who had seen people shot in the streets of Santiago. This priest was really a gift from Heaven. His fighting spirit came to life, and every obstacle on the road to his authorship was just something to be overcome.

Artemio Sandoval had to control himself and handle this energy that overwhelmed him. He stopped. Nyhavn—he found himself in Nyhavn, which was teeming with people. A gentle sun bathed the old houses and the wooden boats in the canal with light. And the sea and the sky seemed united by the same blue purity.

A child with an ice cream in his hand dashed out of an ice cream store and ran into him. A lump of rose-colored ice cream fell on his trousers. Unaware of it, the child went on to join a flock of other children and their teachers. Without caring about the lump of already melting ice cream on his trousers, Artemio Sandoval thought he was a very lucky man to live in such a wonderful country—a country that had been treating him well ever since he arrived as a shabby refugee. And it was at this point the idea struck him—if the Spanish world rejected him because he lived in Denmark, why not write in Danish? Yes, why not write in Danish for the Danes?

As soon as he got back to his apartment, he went to look in his address book by the telephone. He wanted to talk with Delfín Olmazabal, a Chilean refugee who wrote in Danish and had been successful in publishing a few books.

As soon as the Chilean answered the telephone, Artemio Sandoval came straight to the point. He had decided to write in Danish and would like to get some advice, before getting started, from someone with experience in this area. He neglected to mention his defeat on the Spanish market. What good advice did he have for him?

"Keep on writing in Spanish. Don't write in Danish," the Chilean answered categorically.

Artemio Sandoval found the advice downright irritating when it came from a foreigner writing in Danish himself. "What's the problem?" he asked.

"There isn't just one problem, but a lot of them," the Chilean said with emphasis. "The first problem is the damn debate about foreigners. Editors and the like want you to write about immigration topics—integration, identity, Danes and non-Danes, somewhat-Danish and very-Danish, and God knows what."

"But I couldn't care less about those topics," Artemio Sandoval broke in.

The Chilean laughed. "You can care as much less as you will. But it won't help you. Whatever you write becomes first and foremost a subject for public debate. That's just the way it is. Do you want to hear more?"

Of course Artemio Sandoval wanted to hear more. And the Chilean expounded further with great certainty. Danes were more critical when they read something written by a foreigner. For example, a Dane who made up new words and innovations in speech would be considered creative, but a foreigner, well, it would be because he had not learned correct Danish. A Dane who wrote a loony story would be seen as creative, too, but written by a foreigner the same story became ethnic or un-Danish. And even the little misspellings could constitute proof of not being able to write Danish, and finally the book and the author end up as a sympathetic but failed attempt to become integrated... What do you say to that?"

"I really don't know what to say."

"My advice: write in Spanish. And remember, you will be writing so as to be understood by more than a quarter billion people." Then he added, ironically, the typical Danish regards: "Luck and happiness. Goodbye."

"Thank you. Goodbye," Artemio Sandoval answered, also in Danish, but without any irony.

For a foreigner who had come to Denmark in his adult years Artemio Sandoval possessed some of the best qualifications for throwing himself into a literary project in Danish. First and foremost, he had always loved the Danish language and its metallic, German sound. Admittedly, it was a tricky and difficult language, which, in addition, could only be spoken by a few people in one of the world's smallest countries. But for that very reason he felt that in learning Danish he had come to own a priceless treasure.

He had read a lot of books in Danish and knew more about Danish literature than the average Dane. And the time a Copenhagen paper had held a competition to identify a Danish author from a selection of his work, he won a prize of three bottles of wine.

And yet...fascination with a foreign language was one thing; it was quite another to express yourself artistically in that language. Would he be able to do it? Artemio Sandoval had no doubt. His knowledge of and love for the Danish language made it possible for him to create literature in Danish.

But the more he thought about the reactions of Danes that Delfin Olmazabal had mentioned, the more he understood them. Why should the Danes accept a writer who spoke their language with mistakes and a terrible accent? Why should they understand that you could write a sentence over and over until it was correct?

Not to mention that getting a book published was in reality a harsh competition between many submitted manuscripts. And in a salsa competition, the Colombians would not show much confidence in a salsa-dancing light-haired Dane just out of dancing school.

After only a few days, these considerations converged into a solution as simple as it was logical. And Artemio Sandoval wondered why the Chilean had not thought of it himself. You just had to remove the foreign element from your literary work. Of course, a Danish main character and a Danish pseudonym...and the book would be read as the piece of art it was, with no disturbing conjectures about where the author came from or which ethnic identity he had or did not have.

When this strategy reached its full development, he was surprised the theme for his next book appeared almost by itself. On a visit to Colombia, a Dane would encounter experiences he could never have had in Denmark. The Dane in Artemio Sandoval's book would stand face to face with a reality where none of his democratic and humanistic principles were of the slightest use at all. He would be compelled to struggle against his Scandinavian, welfare-state naiveté as he discovered that the only thing that could keep him alive in the South American hell was cruelty—his own cruelty. And at the end, Artemio Sandoval's Dane would, like one coming back from the realm of the dead, return from Colombia only to find a Denmark where he no longer belonged.

This time he knew the way to the last page of a book. So the obstinate Artemio Sandoval once more set to work. Again he adjusted girlfriends, coffee, music, bedtime, and other things to his writing work.

He looked back on that crazy time when he fought his own private war against authors and the art of writing. So obvious—every form of raving was just an expression of powerlessness.

Now life had a perspective in exactly the same way that his writing aimed at a conclusion. And he was approaching his life's goal the same way the book was approaching the last line. Life and literature mirrored one another.

The dogged Artemio Sandoval stopped writing and reading Spanish—and had it been within his power, he would have completely stopped thinking in his mother tongue, too. Danish—the language of his future was Danish. He analyzed novels, stories, songs, advertisements, newscasts, poems, and historical texts. Each Danish text constituted a challenge to his insatiable linguistic hunger. He practiced constantly and also wrote poems, short tales, or anything whatsoever, which were corrected by Danish friends with a ear for language. And he experienced happy days where he managed to write whole pages without mistakes.

There were still some small problems left, particularly

with word order, prepositions, and those damn word-endings. But his self-confidence was untouched because any Dane with an average education could eliminate these elementary errors from his text in just a few minutes.

Artemio Sandoval grew stronger, as did the book and his mastery of the new language.

It was 1995. One morning he was awakened by the mail slot's usual noisy announcement of correspondence. He went over to the door half asleep and picked up a small package from the floor. He knew by the shape and weight that it was a book.

It was from Bettina, a former girlfriend whom he had long ago left for another woman with less interest in cozy domestic life and more insight into literature.

Walking back to his bed, he opened the package. As expected—a book with a letter from Bettina. "Dear sweet Artemio…" He was already tired of reading it. A renewal of that relationship was out of the question. He skipped to the letter's concluding sentences. "Maybe one of these days we can have dinner, light a few candles, and talk about the old days… and so on? A big kiss, Bettina. PS: Hope you'll like the book."

Such a letter had an inherent problem. It forced him to answer, and he had no time for anything but writing. Irritation made him realize he had a pain in his right wrist again this morning. It was because he preferred to write by hand and with a pencil. A habit, almost a ritual, which helped him concentrate more deeply on his creative work. He closed his eyes and tried to will the pain away.

The question of which Danish pseudonym he would use for the forthcoming book made him forget the pain in his hand. He was unusually fond of old Danish names and could not understand Danes calling their children Jimmy or Maria. During the last couple of days he had been able to boil the choices down to two possibilities—Valdemar Gammelgård and Holger Rasmussen. Which…which of the two sounded best?

Finally he condescended to take a closer look at Bettina's gift. Its title was *Out of the Jungle*. What kind of a silly book was it Bettina had sent him? Tarzan's memoir…? But on the back cover he read about "a Dane's gruesome experiences as a prisoner of Colombian guerrillas." All of it based on a "true story."

At first it took Artemio Sandoval by surprise that he did not know anything about this strange event—a Dane kidnapped in Colombia, his native country! Once more he realized that his preoccupation with writing had the power to cut him off from the world. Then it hit him that the plot of *Out of the Jungle* reminded him of his own novel. He opened the book and began to read.

A Dane who works for a Danish company in Colombia is kidnapped by local guerrillas who demand a ransom. The Dane is hidden in the jungle by his kidnappers. The Danish firm, whose security measures failed completely, begins to play a dangerous double game. Publicly they report doing everything they can to ransom their missing employee, but behind the scenes they try to dicker over the amount of the ransom. The firm not only prolongs their employee's captivity but also puts his life at risk.

Artemio Sandoval read and read and encountered one surprise after another. All too many elements of his own book showed up. Sure, in another form and poorly written. Strange, really strange he had not noticed the news of the kidnapped Dane.

He put the book aside before finishing it and looked up at the ceiling, muddled. Was it actually his own book he was reading in *Out of the Jungle*?

No. Categorically not. In spite of all the striking similarities, it lacked the drama and epic development that his main character could deliver to the reader. *Out of the Jungle* was nothing more than a description of an incident without literary verve. His own main character went through a painful change that transformed him from a naïve, cheerful Dane to a disillusioned and hardened man of the world. This transformation was not found at all in the simpleminded anecdote in *Out of the Jungle*.

Artemio Sandoval shook his head. Case closed. There was only a superficial, trivial, resemblance between the two books. And this would be clear to any more or less intelligent reader.

He took a deep breath and let it slowly out while he realized that for a split second he had felt threatened, gripped by an indefinable fear. How ridiculous! He laughed. Such an inferior book as *Out of the Jungle* could not possibly threaten the work of art he was creating. And the more ridiculous his earlier fear seemed to be, the greater his urge to laugh. One burst of laughter came out after the other in an irresistible chain. He needed to open a window. The cool night air would certainly help him get a grip on himself.

Now he did not laugh any more and an unexpected stillness seemed to have fallen over the entire world. He thought fleetingly that winter made Denmark a silent country, and that cold air was rushing into the room, and therefore it was best to close the window. So he shut the window and, right afterward, he turned around and looked at *Out of the Jungle*, which lay on the coffee table. A second later, he sat down on the floor and burst into tears.

His book was as good as doomed. No matter how well he wrote, it would be inevitably considered an extension of an event reported in the newspapers, like some kind of *Out of the Jungle* number two.

How could reality have reproduced the plot he had created step by step? Unbelievable that it could ever happen. It was clear that life opposed his wishes, worked against him. The struggle to become an author was irrevocably lost.

He kept on crying. And every sob that shook his chest left him more tired and indifferent. It was not only literature he was about to give up, but life itself. Without the motivation to write, he was not motivated to live, either. Suicide, for the first time, seemed to him a viable alternative. Until then he had only felt contempt for people who took their own lives. But now he could easily put himself in their situation and understand their profound indifference to a life that prevented one from living.

What do you want to be when you grow up, little Artemio? And little Artemio would always answer promptly: A writer—when I grow up, I want to be a writer.

To write—to write even a single line now struck him as an absurdity beyond all reason. How was it that he had chained himself to the illusion of becoming a writer? He closed his eyes full of tears and the darkness in their depths drew him in. Suddenly he moved weightlessly and quickly through a host of memories that came to meet him.

He remembered that warm night lying face down on the tiles after completing another Roy Jackson story when, for the first time, he saw himself happy as an author. And the dream had accompanied him ever since.

Artemio Sandoval got up, found pencil and paper, and went back to his place on the floor. Tears ran down his cheeks again when he wrote at the top of the sheet of paper: "The Return of Roy Jackson".

The story began with the galloping Roy Jackson on his way to help his hometown, oppressed by a villain. And the child, who always wrote in the present tense, had probably begun with something like this...Roy Jackson rides his faithful horse Lightning...or, Here is the unbeatable hero Roy Jackson...or, The bandits´ terror, Roy Jackson, and his clever horse Lightning approach the town. Artemio Sandoval continued writing until the realization that he could not recall the exact wording made him stop. It could just as well have been any of these beginnings.

The older man kept staring at the surface of the sheet of white, tear-spotted paper, hoping to find the words used by the small boy to write the story, hoping to understand why he was sitting now on the floor, crying over a broken dream.

And suddenly, there on the white paper he caught a glimpse of the hero Roy Jackson. The glimpse of the drawing gave him a shock. He had not only written, but had sketched, too. Excited, he dried his eyes and held his breath for a moment. Something was going to happen, but he did not know what.

The first stroke he made with the pencil drew Roy Jackson's jaw. That stroke began all his drawings of Roy Jackson. He moved the pencil farther up and the hero's left cheek and forehead appeared. It was as if Roy Jackson was just waiting to be drawn on the white paper. With no difficulty Artemio Sandoval's hand remembered the right movements for the right strokes.

And there stood Roy Jackson, back in town, strong, just, and courageous, wearing his cowboy hat and holding a smoking pistol in his right hand. His left boot rested on the dead villain, who had a bullet hole in the middle of his forehead.

Incredulous, Artemio Sandoval shook his head. For his heart beat the heartbeats of the Colombian boy he had been more than forty years ago. And through the mist in his teary eyes, he saw his mother come into the room, go over to him, bend down, and kiss him lovingly on the head. Then she hugged him and closed her eyes. "One day you'll be a famous writer, my Temito," she said with a dreamy voice and hugged her child closer to her. Temito—his mother's loving way of saying little Artemio.

Artemio Sandoval saw that his mother did not look at the paper on which her Temito had both written and drawn. She did not have time, his mother; she was struggling to keep the poverty-stricken family together. She did not notice that her son liked to write, but loved to draw. She could not have known that for her Temito, the story was just a warm-up for the drawing.

And the child—in that intense moment, the child closed his eyes, too, and dreamed his mother's dream.

The grown-up Artemio Sandoval sat on the floor, looked at his childhood hero, and continued to cry. He did not notice that the day was waning and it was already getting dark in his apartment. For it was winter in Denmark, and the short days take the light out with them quickly.

It has been some years since Artemio Sandoval's unexpected reunion with Roy Jackson. He lives a quiet life. You can often catch sight of him around the Copenhagen lakes, his favorite spot for drawing.

Without haste of any kind, with a tender care that shows time is on his side, he finds a bench along the lakeside and unpacks his drawing materials from the black plastic bag that has accompanied him since his young years in South America. He observes and senses the landscape until a place, a person, or a thing reveals to him a certain uniqueness. And then he begins, calm and collected, to reproduce, stroke after stroke, the uniqueness of the chosen subject on the pad's white surface.

It is by the lakes that he both draws and remembers the Artemio Sandoval who for years struggled against himself and life to become an author. Sometimes he moves his hand and eyes away from the sketching pad and looks at the opposite bank, where he can see clearly the ambling, powerless man who could not be what he dreamed to be.

It is also by the lakes that occasional passersby are surprised when they see this middle-aged foreigner with his sketchpad and his absorbed look. At first glance they imagine the most obvious thing—that he suffers from some kind of madness or other. But they quickly come to the conclusion that he is not mentally disturbed, but just one of those artists who live so deeply in their art that they do not care in the least what people around them think or don't think about them. This perception, as far as it goes, is correct, for Artemio

Sandoval is no longer particularly attentive to how he is perceived. He draws his pictures without paying any attention to the fact that through them he has become a sketch artist. Nor does he strive to break the boundaries of the art of drawing in order to create heretofore-unseen images that will make him famous. He draws for the simple reason that his whole life, just like in a story, converged toward the moment when he realized that he had to draw every day.

Truth be told, Artemio Sandoval's drawings possess a strange ability to evoke comments from viewers, some of whom have said enthusiastically that they are "good" and "absolutely works of genius," others that they are "bad" and could "just as well have been drawn by a child." And when he hears these kinds of comments, whether they praise his work or denigrate it, he just shrugs his shoulders humbly and smiles.

For Artemio Sandoval does not consider his drawings "good" or "bad." For him, first and foremost, they are evidence that people—yes, that all of us have to walk a particular path which is frequently just as long as it is inscrutable before we can embrace our fate.

Zapatito

His head seemed larger than most heads—probably because he was so small and crooked-legged. His face was round like a plate, with crooked features just like his legs. His voice and smile were an apology for his whole being. The poverty and malnutrition of childhood had clearly marked his body and soul. He always stirred a kind of pity in me, which I didn't desire because I really liked him.

It was one of those evenings—with yet another ping-pong match between Tim and me down in the basement of the residence hall, with nerves and muscles firmly resolved to beat your opponent.

Tim and I—we were young in '75, not yet twenty-two years old, and we could reach unheard of heights when battling each other around a ping-pong table.

An inattentive second, a quick-witted glance which catches the other's intention, and you became the winner or loser of a point. Victory or defeat—what an enthralling pendulum!

And then the little man with the plate-face showed up and began observing every one of our reactions, a lively attentiveness shining in his brown eyes.

At first we became a little distracted. We were playing both against each other and for him. And all of a sudden something happened—and we fought hard, imaginatively, as we had never done before. Maybe it was his eyes looking into us while they calculated the best moves. What a battle— one of my life's glorious moments.

Tim won as usual. I dried the sweat from my forehead and shook my head clear like a boxer dealing with yet another hard blow. Tim had taught me to play ping-pong, and even though I beat players every bit as good as he was, I just couldn't manage to beat him.

Unexpectedly, the little man approached the table and

said in terrible Danish that he would like to play one of us. This little man, pot-bellied and bow-legged, certainly didn't look like a ping-pong player.

There was something about the way he spoke Danish that was familiar to me. His politeness, his reserved manner while he waited for one of us to answer…he was Chilean!

To see him play ping-pong was a revelation. It was a little grim Buddha, and yet a true Buddha, elegant and mighty, who stood there with his belly, and a paddle in his hand, and made a complete laughingstock of my master-teacher Tim.

I saw it, and I couldn't believe it. Tim looked like a befuddled child fencing in the air with a paddle. Suddenly it was 21 to 3 and the little man smiled apologetically to his shocked opponent.

When it was my turn to play with him, I knew it was a time to learn, not to compete.

The ugly little Buddha, with his strange Chinese grip on the paddle, mastered the intrinsic dimensions of the game— space, body position, stance, movement, speed, angle, direction, et cetera. When he played you didn't see the challenging look, smart spin effects, exquisite serves, hard smashes, striking backhands—the kinds of things I had seen with keen players. His technique was simply fascinating and brilliant. You couldn't surprise him. He always had plenty of time and could be all over the table at once

For someone like me, ping-pong was one of Denmark's many surprises because I was brought up with the nearly religious conviction that soccer was the only real sport in the world. Of course, I knew there was something called ping-pong. But when I stayed at the residence hall and saw close-up these large Danish guys batting the stupid little ball with an equally stupid little paddle, I found the activity foolish beyond compare. And I thought, well, here was some form or other of European eccentricity, which luckily I had been spared—until Tim insisted on teaching me to play. Burdened with the newcomer's politeness toward the host country and its people, I said yes. And little by little I began to be drawn into the game—mainly because I could share with Danes the feelings usually called forth by competition. Ping-pong was a demanding but exciting way into Denmark, the country I needed to know.

Well, then I began to play regularly with this Chilean ping-pong Buddha. I sweated, receiving his suggestions in Chilean Spanish right into my brain. He could see the hidden strand running between body, psyche, and the game. And he said— You have a weak backhand because you stick to what you can do and don't dare to learn anything new. Or—You don't need to move backwards when your opponent is smashing; he's not going to hit you with a hammer. Or—You handle the paddle as if it weighed kilos. You tense your whole arm like a weight-lifter. Why do you exaggerate?

I worked hard to figure out all the possible surprises of the game. My body fought its way fiercely through space. I attacked one moment and defended myself the next. The white ball itself became the enemy that had to be returned with as much force as possible. It was obvious I had absolutely none of his talent—the ability to make great art seem easy. But I made progress.

It surprised me to discover that his knowledge outside ping-pong was fairly limited. Once he traveled to the second largest city, Århus, to speak about torture in Chilean concentration camps, and afterwards he thought he had been beyond Denmark's borders in an entirely different country! Another time when I wanted to separate from my Chilean girl friend, he said that we were Chileans, and therefore we must never live with a Dane! And then there was his absurd communist partiality for all things Russian. In Russia everybody was happy. All the European languages came originally from Russia. The world would go to pieces without Russian science. UFO's were, of course, Russian, and so on.

But, well, he was my friend and guide with a rare wisdom—in sports and in spirit.

He had, by Chilean standards, a grotesque name—Huenchulay Vonderkirk. Its grotesque quality lay in the play between the natural sounding Indian first name, the grandiose German last name, and his humble and completely mangled appearance.

We were about the same age. But our respective backgrounds were worlds apart. If it hadn't been for our country's agonizing history, which sent both of us to Denmark as political refugees, we would never have known of each other's existence.

The fact is I wasn't greatly liked by the other Chilean refugees who at that time lived in Copenhagen. It was 1975, when political opinions meant much more than they were really worth. Unlike the majority of the resident Chileans, I didn't believe at all in violent revolutions and the dictatorship of the proletariat as the only way to human happiness. The Chileans froze me out. And I didn't care the least bit because I didn't need them.

Huenchulay told me one time that he was frequently criticized by his sectarian party members. They didn't look kindly on his relationship with me. I asked, "And how do you feel about it?"

He shrugged his shoulders, a little apologetically, as was his way, and said, "They don't know you. And they don't know anything about ping-pong." Then he looked at me, "But I always tell them you are my friend, and we play ping-pong together."

That's how he was. Genuine and simple—just like his unique ping-pong talent.

It began in southern Chile in the cellar of the textile factory, where he had worked and been an active communist since he was twelve. He told me that one day he picked up a paddle and discovered it just lay there in his hand completely right.

In the cellar he became the factory's champion. He became the champion in a tournament of factories in the region. He became the champion of the whole province. He went to a tournament in Santiago...and won easily. A true talent was on his way to the pinnacle of the sport. He was looking forward to a magnificent South American tournament in Brazil when a military coup overthrew all of Chile in September 1973.

In the concentration camp, the soldiers hung him up by his feet and kept dunking his head into a barrel filled with human excrement. And then of course he received electric shock in his mouth, testicles, and rectum. All the while they laughed at his Indian appearance and German surname.

After a few gruesome months (and thanks to a visit by human rights organizations and the subsequent publicity), the prisoners got a new commandant, fewer torments, better meals, more space...and a ping-pong table.

It was the camp's new commandant himself, the military academy's ping-pong champion, who had ordered the ping-pong table. One of his first directives (his word was law) was that a ping-pong tournament should be held right away. In the context of the development of the tournament, soldiers and prisoners would participate as equals since sportsmanship superceded any political differences. Prisoners—or soldiers for that matter—who mixed sports and politics during the tournament would bitterly regret it.

During the finals, the soldiers and prisoners rooted like wild animals, the soldiers for the tall and handsome commandant and the prisoners for the little bow-legged prisoner, Huenchulay Vonderkirk.

After the contest, the commandant called Huenchulay into his office.

Clearly in bad humor, the commandant dismissed his guard and said in a harsher tone than usual, "Tell me, Vonderkirk, you led 18 to 5 in the decisive set. Did you lose on purpose...or what?"

The prisoner said cautiously, "No, mi Comandante." And added, "Your technique is a good deal better than mine."

The commandant got furious. "Vonderkirk, you shouldn't hoodwink an officer in the Chilean army. Do you think I'm stupid?" He banged on the desk.

The prisoner answered promptly, "No, mi Comandante, it would never occur to me to doubt your intelligence."

The commandant's rage did not lessen at the prisoner's answer. "Don't try to indulge me, Vonderkirk. I am a soldier, not a child!"

The prisoner looked down at the floor, "I just got a lucky start, mi Comandante."

The commandant was shouting now, "A lucky start! I should put you in a cage for this!"

The prisoner, whose glance was nailed to the floor, said, "May I be allowed to insist, mi Comandante, I got a lucky start. And your spin technique is simply...amazing, yes, amazing, mi Comandante."

The commandant turned his back on the prisoner and said, noting to himself, "Here's the proof. Communists are full of lies."

After that, the commandant and the prisoner played ping-pong as often as they could. And the prisoner never won an entire game against the commandant.

In time, Huenchulay became the prisoners' spokes-person—and sometimes the soldiers' too. Everyone in the concentration camp knew that the commandant listened to Huenchulay during and after the ping-pong games.

And so, far from Chile's concentration camps, here in the resident hall in Copenhagen, I finally could beat Tim, my Danish master-teacher. My hours with Huenchulay had made all the difference. I considered joining a club at one point and making a big deal out of my ping-pong abilities. But then, well, I found something else to do and one day I just stopped playing ping-pong forever.

Huenchulay and I went our separate ways, and we only met each other by chance, sometimes not for years. Every time we met, I felt an indescribable happiness at suddenly catching sight of his plate-like face when I least expected it. Here was my first Chilean friend in Denmark—a true friend who had gone against his political flock for me and in addition to that had initiated me into his knowledge of ping-pong so I was able to develop.

No matter what other obligations I had, I always took time to be with him. We talked about particular games we had played, about great moments we had shared around the ping-pong table. He could remember and describe exactly how I developed my spin technique and made my serves more aggressive and when I stopped moving backwards under an opponent's attack. He never failed to remark that "we" had neglected my backhand, my weakest point, and it was a pity we hadn't taken the time to do something about that. He reproached himself for the responsibility he hadn't lived up to. After all, he was my guide.

I tried to come to his aid, saying that my backhand had already become much better with his help. And, well, "we" would have made it perfect if "we" had given ourselves the time to do it.

And we smiled, satisfied, even though the knowledge that there are things in life that will never be finished encircled us more strongly than ever.

Together with Huenchulay in these random hours, Denmark and the Danes became a giant backdrop, like in an empty theater, where we two sat upon the stage, unconcerned, and shared our distance from everything Danish. We had so much in common. We had been children under the Chilean sky. And now we were Chileans in Denmark. Simple but powerful facts.

Was it five or six years ago I last saw him? I can't really remember. I was walking down Jagt Road on the way to Nørrebro Circle when we suddenly stood across from each other. He stopped, as if paralyzed. I walked over to him while I got the definite feeling something was wrong. His round face was pale. Then he took a step back. "You," he said. "Is it really you?"

I clapped him on the shoulder and asked what was wrong.

"Well...well...," he pressed my hand, "It's just that..."

"What?" I asked.

"I almost don't dare say it," he said, and looked far into the distance at nothing in particular.

"Let's sit down and talk," I said.

We reached the circle, and when we turned up Nørrebro Avenue, he mumbled, "To walk down the street and suddenly meet you—you don't know how happy I am."

We found an old café on a corner, which is now run by a Chinese family. We ordered a table for two. His doctor had told him he shouldn't drink alcohol so he took a sip of his soda and said, "Listen, I heard not too long ago...that...that you were dead!" He tried to smile apologetically, but instead he clutched his head. "I don't understand. You're not dead!"

It was a Chilean (he gave me a name I didn't recognize) who had told him I was dead. This man had not only read it in the paper, but he had also attended my funeral!

Reluctantly, Huenchulay gave me a few details of my own death as he had heard it. But I wasn't really listening to him. A feeling of unreality turned my skin cold. And I thought, maybe I had been long dead after all, and crooked little Huenchulay Vonderkirk, because he had been my first Chilean friend in Denmark, was the only person who could see my wandering lost soul in the streets of Copenhagen.

I looked at Huenchulay, wanting an explanation, but he had none.

Then I looked around. To the left of us sat a man drinking

coffee and smoking. His face and eyes had an empty look, but he was breathing and belonged among the living. Farther down, behind the counter, a young Chinese girl was working with quick, precise movements. She was herself the essence of life. The window to the left of me let me see that the sun was shining outside. On the other side of the street a boy was adjusting his roller skates, right under a sign that said: Holte Lane. And I…I was also among the living. Life unfolded as usual.

"I'm really happy it was all a misunderstanding…and you are still here," he said, hugging me before we parted at Nørrebro Avenue.

I walked toward my apartment. What the hell had happened? Who was the great idiot who came up with the idea that I was dead?

Not more than three months later, I met Abelardo at the corner of Stefans and Nørrebro Avenue, right by Stefans Church.

Abelardo is a Chilean, too. A hard childhood and some years in the resistance movement against Pinochet's dictatorship had equipped him with a sympathetic cynicism and a conspicuous predilection for whiskey. A fine meeting right in the middle of busy Nørrebro Avenue! Political opinions don't separate me from other Chileans these days. We went into a café and drank and talked together.

During a pause he said, "Did you know that Zapatito died a few months ago?"

Zapatito in Spanish means "little shoe." To create and give nicknames is a national sport for Chileans. There are some disgusting nicknames. And "Little Shoe" definitely belonged among the friendlier.

I said that I didn't know who Zapatito was.

Abelardo smiled, "I don't really know what his name was. I just knew him by Zapatito."

"Oh," I said. "And now he's dead?"

"Yes. He had some strange sickness or other for a long time. And then it was all over. Skaal to Zapatito!"

There are not many Chileans in Denmark. And now we were one less. Truly it felt like a loss. I skaaled, too.

"Why was he called Zapatito?" I asked.

"Well, he really looked like a zapatito."

"Looked like a zapatito?"

"Exactly. Have you seen those little children's shoes with round shapes and simultaneously all lopsided...ugly, but how shall I say it...sensitive and humble...do you follow me?

Yes. Now I followed him. "Was his name Huenchulay Vonderkirk, and was he a communist?" I asked.

"He was almost the personification of communism, and yes, I heard he had a totally absurd name like that."

It was him. We had never been together in the company of other Chileans. And so I couldn't have known that the other Chileans called him "Little Shoe"— Zapatito.

Inevitably, I came to realize that Abelardo and I were in the same Chinese restaurant on the Nørrebro Avenue corner where I had my last meeting with Huenchulay. Now we were sitting by the large window that let you glimpse a fragment of a quiet little street off Nørrebro Avenue. And from the same angle as that time with Huenchulay, I could read Holte Lane on the little street's sign. Abelardo was sitting at the exact same spot where Huenchulay had sat and told me what he knew about my death and burial. I could recall him talking about doctors and something about not drinking alcohol any more. My good friend had been sick, very sick. And here was Abelardo telling me he was dead.

For a few seconds I was overwhelmed by the same unreal chill as that time with Huenchulay. And even though I wanted to go out into the street immediately to breathe some fresh air, I couldn't quite pull myself together to do it.

Did Huenchulay want to tell me about his own death

when he told me about mine? Was it just death, this superior force, amusing itself by toying with us poor simple humans?

Huenchulay and I had seen each other seldom, at intervals of years. And still it was as if my Denmark and I had lost something so unique and precious. I took a deep breath and emptied my glass.

"He was a good friend of mine," I said.

"Strange. I don't really know why, but I have a great deal of difficulty imagining you two as friends."

I looked at him helplessly. He would not be able to understand what Huenchulay, Zapatito, meant to me.

Abelardo felt obligated to explain something or other. "Look, Zapatito lived in his own world. And you live in yours. I just can't see any connection between you two. Then he shrugged his shoulders, emptied his glass and added, "What the hell. It doesn't matter—Zapatito's dead now anyway."

Edgardo and Teresa

Where in the hell was the damned keyhole? And the staircase —the lousy staircase had never ever had an electric bulb that worked. Edgardo shook his head. In Chile people thought that gold flowed in the Scandinavian streets...and here he stood trying to find a keyhole from the previous century or he couldn't get into his ruin of an apartment in the middle of Copenhagen.

He finally succeeded in sticking the key into the lock's torturous opening. He concentrated on his right-hand fingers as he tried to find the usual position that coaxed the key into the lock, and when it finally turned, releasing its metallic sound, he laughed to himself. Strange, every time he had downed a few beers, this old lock engaged him in a little hand-to-hand combat.

He closed the door behind him, and then said in an inquiring and lightly singing tone, "Tuquita...?" This was the loving turn of speech he used to say "Little Teresa." And suddenly he caught a glimpse of her as a blurred shape looming toward him with incomprehensible speed. A second later, lightning struck his face with a dry, cracking sound, blinding him. He flew backwards a few steps until his back hit the door.

"Swine!" he heard. Yes, Teresa shouted swine—at him.

As he tried to regain his sight, he remembered the distant time in Chile when the soldiers knocked him around...and when three months ago Teresa, in one of her escalating fits of jealousy, had unexpectedly given him a sock on the nose. He held his nose, his fingers drenched with the unmistakable stickiness of blood.

"Bitch!" he shouted, and tumbled into the living room.

And there stood Teresa at the other end of the room, right in front of the window. He stopped, wiped the blood from his nose with his hand, and with a blood-flecked index finger, he pointed at her: "What did I tell you the last time you hit me?"

"Swine, you horny swine!" she shouted. Now it was a matter of offering resistance, and she grabbed the first object her hands could reach, a book from a pile of books on the windowsill, and threw it at him.

The book struck him on the face, but his anger was greater than the pain, and he didn't give the least sign that he had noticed it. "Mierda!" she said savagely, and snarled, baring her teeth. For a brief moment, she looked like a hunted animal. "Don't you hit me!"

"Don't hit you?" he asked tauntingly and kicked the coffee table that was in his way. The table, along with overflowing ashtrays, a pack of cigarettes, a beer bottle, and glass and other items flew through the air, scattering debris everywhere. He took a few more ominous steps toward her. "This time you'll really get to learn something!"

"Keep back—back!" She tried to move backwards but only bumped against the radiator immediately behind her. When she braced both palms against the woodwork of the window frame, she felt a pain in her right wrist. She had promised not to hit him again, but she didn't harbor the least doubt he deserved the sock on the nose.

"You've probably broken it, bitch!" He cautiously felt his nose, which was still throbbing painfully and dripping blood. Without removing his eyes from her, he methodically wiped his bloody hands on his pants.

Teresa read his eyes. She had received that dark look before, and she knew what would soon be triggered. Then she suddenly turned her body and with a lightning-quick movement she flung the window open wide. And she turned toward him again, challenging. "Faggot!" she said, with the greatest contempt, "A real macho doesn't hit women."

Faggot! Boiling with rage, Edgardo took a deep breath through his nose, swallowing some of his own blood. He coughed and spat out a gruel of snot and blood onto his shirt and the floor, and then went quickly toward her. But before he could even see it, Teresa had crawled up on the windowsill.

He stopped—an arm's length from her. "What are you doing?" he asked, dumbfounded. A single wrong movement and she could fall.

"I'll jump!" she said. "I mean it, and it will be your fault!" With only one hand gripping the old, brittle window frame, she leaned her body out toward the empty space—and the asphalt of the street, four stories down.

"Stop that!" he commanded, but with no strength in his voice. He lifted his hand to touch her knee and had almost reached it when she shouted, "I'll jump! Get back!"

Edgardo moved cautiously backwards.

"I don't give a damn!" She sat tense, staring and squatting like an enormous spider on the windowsill. "I've been drinking," and then she added menacingly, "and I've taken speed."

"Haven't I told you I don't want you to do that?" Now he showed as much anger as worry.

"I'll jump!" She sat down carelessly on the windowsill, her back supported by the window frame, one leg resting on the sill itself and the other hanging out over the chasm. She leaned her body and her head out and stared down. "I'll kill myself. I will!"

"No," he mumbled impotently. "No…"

"Yes! Because you don't give a damn about me." Without holding on to anything at all, she leaned her body out a few more centimeters. If her body's weight pulled her off the windowsill, she would fall, hit the pavement, and probably die on the spot.

"Tuquita," he implored. "Come on in now."

She straightened up, back to a stable position on the windowsill, and looked at him.

A thin, dark red line of blood ran out of one of his nostrils. His nose, in any case, was not broken—and that both relieved her and made her angrier. "Who were you with this evening?" she asked.

"Oh, stop it, Tuquita. You know very well I was at a solidarity meeting."

"Lies! The meeting was over hours ago. Do you think I'm an idiot or what? You were with some..."

He interrupted: "After the meeting I went to a bar with Juan and Temo." And unexpectedly he bellowed, "Come down from there, you dumb bitch!"

Her answer was short and precise, "On your knees."

"What?"

"Get down on your knees."

He gave her a furious look.

Her eyes gripped his. "Do you think I won't jump—do you?"

Edgardo had seen her this way before. It was best to obey. He knelt.

"Say you are a swine," she commanded.

"Okay," he said, dejected. "I'm a swine."

"A horny swine. Say you're a horny swine!"

"I'm a horny swine."

"Louder!"

He raised his voice." I'm a horny swine!"

"And I'm completely wild about the Danish bitches."

He raised his eyes toward the ceiling, shook his head in disbelief, and assumed an exaggerated, hopeless expression.

Small drops of spit flew out of her mouth when she shouted, "Say it!"

"Okay, okay," he said and indicated his consent by raising his hands. "Yes, I'm completely wild about the Danish bitches." He paused and said pleadingly, "Please come back in now. Come on, Tuquita." He made a movement to rise.

"I'll jump if you get up!" She moved her whole body outward, just a little, but dangerously convincing.

"Why are you doing this?" he asked. "My knees hurt and I want to wash my face."

"Oh, the great man's knees hurt?" she asked, mocking and taunting him. "And he wants to wash his face."

"Tuquita," he said gravely, "You know I don't like you taking pills. Come on down now."

"Are you still going to hit me?"

"No, I won't hit you." And thereafter he tried to sound as calm and natural as possible. "Hop in now. It's time to go to bed." Again it seemed he was about to stand up.

"Don't get up," she warned. "I'll jump, I'll jump!" She turned her head and body toward the darkness outside as though she would jump any second.

"No, Tuquita, I'm not getting up." He asked submissively, "What is it you want me to do?"

She seemed to ignore his question. And suddenly she looked just like some attractive Latin girl in a flowered dress, sitting on a park bench with plenty of time to look at the city and to remember everything and nothing. A couple of times she shook her head pensively as if she couldn't convince herself about just what she saw or remembered.

He grimaced; now his knees caused him more pain than his nose. He tried to reach her. "You know I love you. Come on down now and let's forget all this."

At last she reacted—with renewed aggression. "You're full of lies. You won't forget."

"Come on in, Tuquita. I don't want you to get hurt."

"Say you won't hit me because I hit you on the nose."

"No, I won't hit you because you hit me on the nose," he promised, pronouncing the words distinctly. "I mean it."

"I don't want you to mean anything." Her commanding forefinger corrected him, "You have to promise it."

"Yes, Tuquita," he hurried to say, "I promise."

"What do you promise?"

"I promise I won't hit you because you hit me on the nose."

"You said earlier you would hit me."

"That was just something I said. Come on in now. Let's stop all this nonsense."

"I don't know," she said and tried to read his eyes. "I can't tell whether you mean it."

"Yes, of course I mean it. Come on in."

A moment passed without words. "Okay," she said suddenly. "Okay." And as if there hadn't been any kind of spectacle, she turned her legs in toward the room, and with a perfectly graceful little hop landed on both her feet on the floor.

He let out a sigh of relief and with difficulty began to stand up.

Wrapped in thought, without glancing at him once, she started searching for the ashtray, the matchbox, and the pack of cigarettes that had taken the flying tour with the kicked coffee table. At last she gathered everything up. And she was calmly and quietly on her way over to the sofa to sit down and light a cigarette, when he stretched out his left hand and grabbed her by the hair.

"Ouch!" she cried out and dropped everything on the floor.

"You dirty bitch!" He yanked her to him. "Do you think you can threaten me?" By turning his wrist, he forced her to look up at him.

"You faggot," she answered. "You promised..." But she didn't get to complete the sentence. A hard slap in the face by an open hand knocked her down.

"I'll teach you to threaten me!" His hand gripped her hair again and pulled her whole body up.

Everything around her had turned blurry and her head was humming. Still she mumbled a curse and kicked him in the shin with the toe of her shoe. But he showed absolutely no sign of feeling anything at all. And more slaps rained on both sides of her head. She fended off his blows with her hands as best she could. But the last blow, harder than the others, sent her reeling to the floor again.

In an instant he straddled her. With a knee on each of her outstretched arms, she found it impossible to resist. He lifted his right hand as if to strike her again and said, stressing each word, "Say after me…I will never again threaten to jump out the window."

Her face had begun to swell up. And the weight of his knees created a brutal pressure on her arms. Sobbing, she said, "Okay, Gualito! I'll never threaten to jump out the window again!" Gualito was the affectionate way she used to say Little Edgardo.

His rage didn't seem to lessen. "I can't hear you!" The open hand lifted, turned outward, fell and struck her face relentlessly. "Are you going to do it again?"

"No, Gualito…no!" She tossed her head and flinched with tear-filled eyes, her only defense against the punishing hand. "I didn't mean it!"

"If you ever do something like that again, you'd better jump out the window once and for all!" He grabbed her jaw and forced her to look at him. "Because the next time you do that, I'll knock you to hell and beyond, and then I'll fling you down onto the street myself." His hand lifted, ready to strike her again. He asked, "Is that understood?"

"Yes, Gualito…never again," she promised. "I'll never do it again." She was nearly nailed to the floor and raised her head a few times, attempting to nod affirmatively.

For a short moment, he observed her with wide-open eyes and quivering lower lip, not knowing what he should say or do. Then his tense fingers began to open her dress, button after button, and when he finished, he took hold of her pants at her hips to pull them off.

Now she could finally move her cramped arms. She put her hands on his shoulders and helped him by lifting her buttocks and bending her legs up one by one so the pants could be pulled all the way off.

With firm movements he unbuckled his belt and pushed his pants down. She spread her legs and took hold of his already stiff prick. Then, with her usual confidence, she reached between his legs and guided his prick up into her.

His first thrust met her groin halfway, which had lifted when she energetically pulled her buttocks together. And they continued like that…

They remained lying on the floor, on their backs, side by side, surrounded by the gentle silence of the summer night. She fumbled with her hands, found the cigarettes and matches she had dropped on the floor several minutes earlier.

They lit cigarettes, smoked, and flicked the ashes on the floor. His nose was puffy, and coagulated blood spotted his face and clothes. Her cheeks were red and swollen; a single blue shadow underlined her left eye.

Above them, the wide-open window brought refreshing waves of fresh summer air into the apartment. Another one of these strange, all too early, Danish dawns was about to break through.

She said calmly and without a hint of confrontation, "You promised you wouldn't hit me."

And he answered, just as composed, "I didn't hit you because you hit me in the nose, but because you threatened to jump out of the window."

"You didn't want me to jump, then?"

"No, I didn't."

"Do you still have feelings for me?"

"You know I do."

They turned back to their mutual silence. Many more dancing whirls of smoke spiraled toward the ceiling and more ashes were spread on the floor. Their eyes rested on the wide-open window, which revealed the Danish morning sky, its depth and its light—as distant and incomprehensible as usual.

At last she buttoned her dress and sat up on the floor. He remained lying there, blood-flecked and with pants and underwear still down around his knees. She looked at him, sighed despairingly and asked, "What's happened to us?"

Now it was he who sighed despairingly. He pulled his pants up and sat down, flicked his ashes on the floor, took a deep puff on his cigarette and let the smoke slowly trickle out of his mouth. He said, "Yes. What's happened?" Then he looked up at the ceiling and blew, nearly spat, the rest of the smoke out of his lungs. "What's happened is what has happened—that which should happen, don't you think?"

She shook her head, both denying and remembering. "We weren't the way...we are now. I can't understand it."

"Once and for all you have to understand," and he raised his voice a little. "Chile is far, far away. And gets farther away every day we are here."

"I know it," she said. "Don't you think I know it?"

"It looks like you forget it every time."

She found the ashtray, not far from her hand, and put out her cigarette. He put out his cigarette, too.

She explained. "I'm not thinking about Chile. I'm thinking about us, about the time we were students, when we met in the party, when we passed out leaflets together...we had just fallen in love and we believed in the future...before we came here."

"It's the same thing," he said, with a tinge of irritation.

"What's the same thing?" she asked and tried to find the answer in his eyes.

"That Chile is far away. That there was a time we met in the party and believed in the future. It is all the same."

"Oh, yeah," she said, "yeah, that's probably right." She lit a cigarette and gave it to him. After that she lit one for herself.

"Do you still love me?" she asked.

"You know I do," he answered.

"You never hit me in Chile."

"No. And you didn't, either."

"I'm not unfaithful to you. I know you do all kinds of things on the side. You and your friends...I know you can't resist Danish women."

"Stop it now. Don't start all that again."

"Why should you be different than the others? Most of our friends have gotten divorced. And it's not the women who leave. It's you, the men. So then I just think about when you'll leave me for a Dane."

"Don't be thinking that way. You know I'm not going anywhere."

"Do you have another woman…on the side?"

"Now you're making me tired."

"I can see you don't want to talk about it."

"I don't want to because you have asked me the same thing hundreds of times."

"Can't you understand that I'm insecure?"

"Certainly. But I *will* clear out if you keep on drinking and taking pills. You're getting crazy. And you know very well I don't like it."

"I don't like it, either."

"Is it your friend, the nurse, you were taking speed with?" he asked without expecting an answer.

"Yes," she answered.

"She's bad company, that one," he said dryly. "I've told you I don't think you should see her any more."

"Your friends are bad company, too. I don't think you should see them any more," she said in the same tone.

"Let's not begin all over again." And after a short pause, he said abruptly, "Now let's go to bed."

"Yes," she answered gently and smiled expectantly.

He smiled, too, and kissed her on the mouth, long, lovingly. Then he got up and walked toward the square meter of a bathroom they had in the entryway.

She got up, too, closed the window, lit a new cigarette and began to slowly and carefully remove her jewelry: her earrings, some necklaces, and an armband were laid on a shelf. And it was when she had just stepped into the bedroom and had already unbuttoned two buttons of her dress that the telephone rang.

Surprised, she stopped and looked questioningly at the phone.

The phone rang a second time and he came out of the toilet bare-chested. "Who the hell can that be so late." His wristwatch showed it was nearly four A.M. "Just let it ring," he said, uninterested.

The telephone rang for a third time.

"What if it's my mother, from Chile?" she asked.

He shrugged his shoulders. "She just called last week. Let's go to bed," he concluded and went back into the bathroom again.

When the telephone rang for the fourth time, she picked up the receiver. "Hello," she said.

"Hello," said a woman's voice, in perfect Danish. "Is Edgardo there?"

"Who are you?" Teresa said sharply.

But the only answer she got was the sound of the telephone hanging up on the other end.

She looked helplessly at the mute telephone and hung it up. Suddenly she felt the need for fresh air and opened the window again. She stood there by the window with only her cigarette for company.

The smoke coming out of her mouth dissolved almost instantly in the morning's infinity of space, light, and fresh air. In spite of this, she still felt the thick, stifling heat of the apartment. Copenhagen and its old buildings seemed lost in an indifferent sleep of ages. And the clear light of that night without a night reflected tenuous gleams in the bricks of the walls and the oxide green of the roofs and towers. She shook her head...yes, she shook her head a number of times.

In the meantime, Edgardo had finished his preparations for the night, and came out of the bathroom naked, tired, and sleepy. The moment he stepped into the hall, he rubbed his eyes and said in a lightly singing tone, "Tuquita?" When he took his fingers from his eyes, he saw her dark hair, her face, the upper part of a half-open flowered dress...all looming toward him. And lightning, which struck his face and exploded in an enormous flash, took his sight from him.

"You horny swine!" shouted Teresa, near and far away at the same time.

As a reflex, he felt his nose, and his fingers touched a familiar stickiness.

"Dirty bitch! You dirty bitch!

Edgardo's voice could be heard all the way into the living room, where Teresa, right in front of the open window, waited for him, armed with a book in her hand.

The Trail We Leave

A barrier was removed, and two stewardesses efficiently set themselves up behind a counter. The plane was ready to receive its impatient passengers.

As for me, well, better to pay more, miss something, be annoyed afterwards, than to stand in line and be reminded with every slow little step that, when all is said and done, you are nothing more than an insignificant part of the herd and have to adjust yourself to its pace. I intended to wait, entrust my tired body to the comfortable airport chair until I could go directly to the plane.

The young Danish girl I had met a few days ago in Gonzalo's café suddenly rushed into the transit hall. She stopped, winded and confused, and looked everywhere and nowhere simultaneously. At last she caught sight of the enormous queue of passengers and went right over. She staggered forward while she dragged one of the largest backpacks I have ever seen. I wondered whether she would be allowed to board the plane at all with that Bedouin tent on her back.

Before she showed up, I had asked myself repeatedly what could have become of her. Now she was here, and soon our eyes would meet. At Gonzalo's café the Danish girl had told me that her trip through Latin America had begun a whole year ago, many thousand kilometers to the north, in Mexico. And in Denmark, before departing, she had determined the time and place for her return—today, from Santiago. We had laughed. My trip to Chile had begun "only" three weeks ago. What a coincidence that we should be traveling together back to Denmark!

What was the name of this wholesome Danish girl? Was it Jette…? Mette…? Merethe…? In any case, something like that.

It was Gonzalo who introduced me to the four young

Danes, three girls and a guy, who sat at one of the café tables. We shook hands and then drank heavily the rest of the night. I could remember two names out of the four, but not this girl's.

Around four in the morning, Gonzalo closed the café, and all six of us drove around in Santiago's night, jammed together in his elegant Mercedes Benz. We tried to get into various Santiago nightclubs, but even the common dives with striptease and cheap salsa were swarming with people. Chile's economic progress made itself evident at night, too.

So we ended up at Gonzalo's house, where he proudly played popular Danish music from the seventies on an old Bang and Olufsen stereo. And there was suddenly the music and songs that once had received us in Denmark.

Café and restaurant owner Gonzalo now and then was overcome by that kind of sentimentality that locates "the good old days" at the end of 1974, when we were a part of a tiny band of Chileans who had their first experience of exile in Århus. When we held meetings with our Danish neighbors in Grøfthøj Park, when we learned to speak Danish, when we celebrated our first New Year in Denmark…and so on—all of that was the good old days.

At one point when the Danes, the guy and the three girls, danced helter-skelter around a Christmas tree like drunken blond children, he said thoughtfully to himself and to me, "They are good people. They really are."

He was speaking of both the dancing Danes in his apartment and of all Danes of all times. His inebriated glance sought some kind of affirmation from me. That made me nod in agreement. And then he clapped me on the shoulders so I would not forget what he intended to tell me. He said, "And they treated us two…and all the other ass-holes…so well."

The other ass-holes were the other Chilean refuges. Gonzalo is one of the many former refugees who speaks disparagingly of his earlier, political comrades. On the other hand, he is one of the few who succeeded in returning to the old country and becoming well-off.

The Danish girl and I made eye contact and waved to each other. To remain sitting could convey a gesture of indifference I definitely did not feel. And I was about to get up and go over to her and the queue of passengers, when I heard a woman's voice over the loudspeaker saying something like: "El Señor Héctor Alberto Zurita Alfaro, en el sector tránsito, diríjase por favor a policía internacional, que lo espera a la entrada del sector."

I thought at first my hangover was fooling me and mixing memory and reality in my head because the loudspeakers had just called Héctor Zurita, my school comrade for seven years. From the age of ten until we left high school as seventeen-year-olds, Zurita and I shared classrooms at the Instituto Nacional, the oldest educational institution in Chile.

Full names in Spanish consist of—at least—two first names and two last names. A person's first and second surname are always the father's and mother's first surname respectively. The exact duplication of names is extremely unlikely. In this case both surnames and both first names were called out. It could be no one but Zurita, my school comrade.

According to the announcement, Zurita, who clearly found himself in the same locale as me, had to report to the airport's international police—a special airport unit.

This confused me. I had not seen Zurita since we left high school and now, a quarter of a century later, fate had brought us within a few meters of each other in this airport.

I saw Zurita's face before me. His teasing green eyes. The pink skin and the delicate, beautiful features. I heard his voice—a touch high, fragile as his whole being. I saw him with a striking clarity, around eleven or twelve years old, on his way into the classroom with his elegant and casual style, giving the impression that he went around dressed in something completely different than the school uniform's anonymous blue blazer, white shirt, blue tie, gray pants, and black shoes.

I don't know why, but in dreams or in random memories, which now and then crowd into the present, I always picture my school comrades around eleven or twelve years old. If I want to remember them at another age—say fifteen, sixteen, or seventeen—then I have to strain and consciously search the depths of my memory. The thought has struck me that I have difficulty remembering the years of our youth because it was there that life's sharp blows fell.

Yes, when Zurita was a boy of eleven or twelve, he already looked like a man of the world, walking up and down the countless halls and stairs of the Instituto Nacional, as if high school life were no more than an obligatory but indifferent circumstance.

Otherwise we all resembled small men. We grew up in a time that wanted to turn boys into men quickly. As is the custom in Chilean schools, students always referred to each other by their last names. First names were only found in the school register. If we spoke to a teacher, it was always "usted." The teachers could, of course, say "tú" to a student, but they always used "usted" in order to maintain a distance, and, mainly, to fulfill the demand to squash childhood as soon as possible.

History teacher Señor Salazar: "Palma, I thought that stupidity had limits, but after your answer, I have revised my opinion."

General Inspector Señor Montano: "Palma, your sloppy way of wearing the Instituto Nacional's uniform is a disgrace. You'd better understand this, or find yourself another educational institution." And there I was, wondering why my shoes got dirty and my pants wrinkled so quickly.

Zurita united negligence and formality. I'm convinced that General Inspector Señor Montano never corrected him even though fairly often his tie was crooked or his smart shoes were of brown suede, not of black leather, as the regulations prescribed.

Small, anonymous, uniformed men we were, while Zurita radiated individuality and style. In any case, his dissertation was clear proof of this.

It was in seventh grade. In Spanish class we all had to give a lecture on a famous person. The teacher judged every single student's presentation. Like everything else that involved all the students in the class, the round of dissertations were spread out over weeks and in alphabetical order according to the first surname's beginning letter. So Zurita was the last one who stood before the class, delivering a famous person's life and accomplishments.

And Zurita spoke while he walked back and forth, relaxed. Not only that, he also gestured with his hands to emphasize important points and looked around the room when he paused. Prior to his presentation, we had all stood stiffly as if nailed fast to the floor, without gestures, and, nervous, locked our eyes on an invisible point on the back wall of the classroom. The class was taken by surprise. An eleven-year-old student behaving like a teacher!

The teacher interrupted our giggles and snickers, threw a couple of students out of class, and declared pointedly that we were a bunch of boors who didn't understand the value of Zurita's abilities. This is how a dissertation should be done. Zurita's smile told us he had expected the teacher's reaction and was enjoying the comeuppance we got.

Zurita (and I) never ranked among the ten best of the class's forty students. In our elite high school there was little sympathy for average performances. The remaining thirty were called with undisguised contempt "el montón"—the heap. Furthermore, he was also a poor gymnast—his body showed neither suppleness nor strength.

But Zurita had what the Chileans call "chispa"—spunk. You have chispa if you can show originality—break through the usual modes of thought. He showed chispa the time he made fun of Quezada, the class's most passionate communist. It must have been early in our adolescence, when we were about fifteen.

During one of the breaks, Quezada was going full tilt declaring that all of us would be in charge of the exploitation of Chile's impoverished masses. The education we got at the Instituto Nacional had only this evil purpose. His well-known dramatizing was escalating without consideration of the audience, which had already had enough of his ideological declarations.

Suddenly Zurita went over to him and shook his hand. With his free hand, he clapped Quezada enthusiastically, appreciatively, on the shoulder.

Quezada's verbal waterfall stopped. He was speechless and confused—suddenly caught in the middle of an unexpected praise and an unexpected interruption. Then Zurita said, as though Quezada was already finished with his grandiose oration, "Good! Really good! Man, I'm in complete agreement with you!" Unfazed, Zurita kept on clapping the speechless Quezada appreciatively on the shoulder. "Man, I'm in complete agreement with you!"

For a second Quezada thought, like us, that his oratorical skills were really being appreciated, but that Zurita had made a mistake, for the speech was not really finished yet. Then we all broke into laughter—even Quezada, who suddenly realized his lack of restraint in his political speeches.

We had been unable to liberate ourselves from Quezada's torturous effusions. And then Zurita gave him short shrift with a few words of praise, a squeeze of the hand, and a few claps on the shoulder—so merciless and so elegant.

For the rest of the school year, no one could engage in any argumentation that went on too long. Speakers saw the need to limit time and body language in order to avoid being cut off by one of the listeners with a squeeze of the hand, a clap on the shoulder, and the message, "Man, I'm in complete agreement with you!"

Still another proof of Zurita's chispa was the question, "In the morning or in the afternoon?" that began with the history teacher's vivid description of the Battle of Thermopylae in ancient days between Leonidas' brave handful of Spartans and King Xerxes´ thousands of Persians. A Persian messenger had tried to convince Leonidas he might just as well surrender immediately. As an argument for this, the messenger stated something like they, the Persians, would shoot so many arrows at them, the Greeks, that the sky would go dark. Fearless Leonidas said something like, well, that would be wonderful because Spartans fought better in the dark.

This genuine macho answer created admiration among the forty boys in the class. The teacher, who was certainly well acquainted with such a reaction, fell silent a few seconds so we could enjoy the beauty of the episode.

Zurita requested permission to say something by raising his hand. The teacher nodded affirmatively, and then Zurita rose and broke the solemn silence by asking, "Was it in the morning or in the afternoon?"

More than 2000 years later, it was completely inconsequential whether Leonidas had given his famous answer in the morning or in the afternoon. How could he think of asking such an absurd question? Not even the school's strong discipline kept us from nearly dying of laughter.

The teacher, who saw his historic report shot down with laughter, asked Zurita to stand up again.

"Such a stupid question must have a very special reason," he said and waited.

"I apologize, Señor. I asked without thinking," Zurita answered promptly but with feigned innocence.

The following months the question repeated itself in innumerable contexts. For example, someone would be telling a bunch of interested listeners how he felt up a young girl under her skirt. In the middle of the most exciting part, when his eager fingers were nearing her underpants, he would be interrupted by one of his listeners and asked the anticlimactic question, "Was it in the morning or in the afternoon?"

This question had the strange ability to destroy the dynamic of any story and, moreover, make a fool out of the storyteller. It ended up that some of us introduced any exciting incident we wanted to tell by emphasizing a fortuitous time of day—"...and, okay, okay, it happened in the afternoon." In that way you could be sure your story would not be destroyed by laughter later on.

Zurita—this fragile and brilliant boy, who, with outrageous effectiveness, could scuttle the drama and solemnity in everyday life. I found it difficult to understand when I learned he had become one of the leaders of the resistance against Pinochet's military dictatorship.

At the end of 1971, Zurita and I and the whole class finished high school. The overriding plan prescribed that we should go to the university and become something, preferably something special, in order to live up to the reputation of the Instituto Nacional and to serve the fatherland. After graduation, I got involved in activities that three years later, in 1974, would bring me to Denmark. And like clouds scattered by a powerful wind, the old classmates vanished from my life.

It was the end of 1983, I think, nearly twelve years since I had last seen Zurita, that I read in a Chilean paper sympathetic to the dictatorship that the long sought Héctor Alberto Zurita Alfaro, military leader of Chile's largest terrorist organization, had finally been captured by the security forces. After an intense shoot-out, he lay seriously wounded in an emergency room in Santiago. The newspaper further reported that he was twenty-nine years old and a former student of the Instituto Nacional.

Zurita—leader of a resistance movement (and military commander as well) seriously wounded and guarded day and night by armed soldiers. There were some others in my class I could easily imagine in that situation.

For example, Saietz, whose father, I think, was a socialist member of Parliament. He was just as good at karate, weapons, and explosives as he was in Marx, Engels, and Lenin—after one or more trips to Cuba. There was great controversy at the high school when a national newspaper showed Saietz at the side of President Allende with a Kalashnikov in his hands. Was it right or wrong that a student was a bodyguard for the president and went around with a Russian machine gun in his spare time?

Saietz was big, with huge strong hands. He exuded a priest's solemn self-assurance. He argued in a calm and collected manner, as if he spoke to people who were not themselves guilty of an insufficient understanding of surplus value, exploitation, imperialism, and so forth. He had no doubts. He didn't reproach anyone.

For Saietz, the die was already cast. And he would stand up the day that class warfare called. So far as I know, Saietz fell in battle against his own country's soldiers the 11th of September 1973, the day when the military coup took place. Saietz's fate would not surprise anyone.

But I was greatly surprised by Zurita's spectacular career. In any case, I could not imagine his frail voice ordering acts of sabotage or his equally frail hands gripped around a pistol.

Some years later, in 1988 or 1989, I do not remember exactly, I read in a Chilean paper that the terrorist leader Héctor Zurita had again been seriously wounded, this time in Santiago's prison in a knife fight between political and common, criminal prisoners.

The loudspeakers repeated the message. Now I had to abandon my memories and turn my attention to the fact that Zurita and I found ourselves near each other in the same airport. I got up without knowing why I did. The Danish girl, still in the moving line of passengers, smiled at me.

Confusion made me wave to her. Thoughts swirled in my head.

Zurita had to be on his way out of the country. Why else would he be in this transit hall? But the airport police were summoning him. Perhaps he was trying to get out of the country illegally...and had been discovered. In 1983 he was thrown in prison for activities for which he could easily receive a death sentence. It would be strange if only 14 years later he was allowed to leave Chile just like any other normal passenger.

I know my country. The loudspeaker's extremely well modulated and polite request to report to the airport police meant plainclothesmen were already looking for Zurita. It could well be he was already on the way to the airport police of his own free will. But they would look for him, like relentless bloodhounds, until they found him.

On the other side of the huge window, airplanes parked out on the tarmac told me I was at the last gate. I turned and looked toward the other end of the transit hall. Someplace or other down there was my school comrade Zurita.

I left my carry-on luggage on a chair and began to walk toward the other end of the transit hall. The Danish girl looked surprised. I had gotten up and waved, but instead of going over and keeping her company in the queue, I was moving away from her and the queue that led onto the plane and back to Denmark.

I had to find Zurita, talk with him before the airport police found him. It was an impulse I could not resist.

In glimpses I remembered that in 1984, I myself had an unpleasant little tour with the airport police, who at that time were a section of the dictatorship's secret police. I had not been in Chile since leaving in 1974. A kind of amnesty law had previously given thousands of Chilean exiles the possibility to see their country again. As soon as my Danish passport was stamped, a button under the counter was pushed, and plainclothes police asked me to follow them. My Danish common-law wife, who had gone to Chile ahead of me, and was waiting in the arrival hall, became afraid and started asking the airport and airline personnel what had happened to me. I was the only passenger who had not come into the arrival hall. The police who detained me observed her efforts through a window. After an unpleasant interrogation, some signatures here and there, and a reminder that any unfriendly act toward the regime would cost me dearly, they let me go. Certainly, if she had not made a fuss, they would have held me much longer.

Now I thought that my mere presence could help Zurita. Having a witness to a politically motivated arrest puts a kind of pressure on the power structure that can help the one arrested. Chile was no longer a dictatorship, but Zurita's case could bring out the worst in the police. His activities in the resistance had mainly targeted the police and the military.

Then there were also other possible scenarios. For example, Zurita could give me a telephone number I could call and inform someone about his arrest in the airport. I was ready to go a long way to help him.

Deep down I hoped for the best possible situation—that he was leaving Chile in a lawful manner and that the loudspeaker's call for him was just the result of a trivial formality. In that case, I would give him a comradely clap on the shoulder like when we were students at the Instituto Nacional, and I would wish him luck and happiness—two things he clearly did not have a lot of.

The remains of my hangover, which had accompanied me to the airport, dissolved in my restless pacing through the transit hall. And suddenly it occurred to me I was searching for a joyful and teasing Zurita around eleven years old and in school uniform. He was now, like me, in the beginning of his forties. And a long prison term, plus the accompanying torture and the two times he had been seriously wounded, could not possible have made him look too good.

I moved through the hall faster and faster, while I screened out children, teenagers, old men, and all the women. Minutes flew by. Not one of the men I scrutinized could have been Zurita.

I was looking for some peculiarity or other, something disturbing the usual airport atmosphere—for example, a group of three men, where the man in the middle had a furrowed brow and the two others were strong, efficient, very well-dressed with weapons bulging under their jackets, or a man, bowed over and resigned, not waiting to embark on a plane but rather to be discovered and led off. A man who both was and was not the class comrade I remembered. I was searching for a mystery.

How could Zurita have ended up in the guerrilla world? A world that feeds on binding solemn vows and dangerous dramatic situations.

At some point or other, Zurita must have heard a call, and he abandoned the comfortable distance from which he ridiculed others' engagement and entered fully into the surrounding world at the risk of his own life. And he no longer made others laugh and distance themselves from daily life. Instead, he now pushed them to take extreme positions; to sentence enemies and traitors in their own ranks to death; to show courage and sacrifice in acts of sabotage, gun battles and the like; and to live with the prospect of being tortured or killed at any moment.

A military chief in such an organization is often thought of as a born leader. But Zurita, in spite of his brilliant and infectious sense of humor, never became a leader the others in the class admired. In the first place, the leadership of individual students was an unknown phenomenon in our high school. In the second place, he had a delicate physique and casual manner. The third and most crucial reason was that he never showed the least interest in being anyone's leader.

A real transformation must have taken place to make Zurita the model for whom the rank and file members of his organization felt the mobilizing blend of admiration and respect. Perhaps what I call a transformation was nothing but certain powers that had lain hidden within him, just waiting to be expressed.

Perhaps there was neither transformation nor a power within him, but only the everlasting demands of the Instituto Nacional on its students, that made a guerilla leader out of Zurita. Many of Chile's presidents and innumerable key people in politics, arts, science, and so on, had studied at the Instituto Nacional, whose students achieved the highest averages in college entrance exams every year. We were constantly beaten over the head about all the greatness we should live up to. And Zurita, the teasing boy, had undoubtedly become something special.

I reached the other end of the transit hall without once catching sight of a single man that might be Zurita. I stopped and looked around. I had to find my class comrade before the others found him.

I noted anxiously that I could not see the queue to the plane nor calculate how much longer I could afford to search for him. In a few minutes the gate to the plane would be closed.

My plane...it occurred to me that when I decided to find Zurita I took it for granted that he was not among the passengers flying with me. The reason was simple; Denmark has never been a place for prominent Chilean guerrilla leaders. Italy, France, even Sweden, are the appropriate countries.

Therefore, I had not considered any of the people in my waiting area or in its queue. And now I was standing at the other end of the transit hall. But my plane was not on the way to Denmark. I was on the way to Denmark. My plane was on the way to Paris, where I had to change planes for Copenhagen.

But you never think logically when you most need to. At the moment the loudspeakers paged Zurita, he could very well have been nearby or in the queue, like the Danish girl, and on his way to Paris.

I had to pull myself together. The first thing that hit me was the loudspeakers had not repeated the message. And this could mean Zurita, of his own free will or not, had already reported to the airport police at the entrance to the transit hall. I hurried over there.

The entrance—just a few steps from me travelers' passports were thoroughly examined and stamped. Farther down, at the back of the room, the queue leading to my flight was now only a couple of meters long. The Danish girl was standing on her toes, scanning the people swarming in the rest of the transit hall. She was probably trying to catch sight of me, but could not imagine that I stood close to her now, next to the passport control.

Two plainclothes policeman, with their threatening Latin American appearance, stood guard in front of a door while they carefully observed the passengers coming into the transit hall. The door was hardly distinguishable from the one I had gone through in 1983. If Zurita was nearby, then he could only be behind that door.

On purpose I did not give myself any time to think about it, but went over to the policeman standing right in front of the door and said, "Hello. There was a man paged over the loudspeakers. His name is Héctor Alberto Zurita Alfaro." He wrinkled his forehead and squinted. He knew very well what I was talking about. And he also knew very well that I was not Zurita.

The man remained motionless, just like his colleague, for all too long a time for my nerves. Then he asked me with exaggerated distinctness, "And...are you Héctor Alberto Zurita Alfaro?"

The sound of his question was like a blow in the face. It meant "And what has that to do with you?"

I answered, "No, but I heard his name over the loudspeakers. I know him and thought that..."

He interrupted me. As before, he moved only his lips. "And…are you Héctor Alberto Zurita Alfaro?"

Again I felt the blow of the question. This time he spoke louder, and the warning tone said that now for my own sake I had better go about my business. If it had been during the time of the dictatorship, I would immediately have joined Zurita and consequently received the same treatment. The days of the dictatorship were past, but the Chilean police still had a great deal of power. And if I kept on sticking my nose into their business, the two officers, with a great many legal clauses supporting them, could easily arrest me.

"I am not Héctor Zurita," I said, "but I want to see him."

For a short moment the man and I looked directly into each other's eyes. The only thing I wanted was to see Zurita. For seven years he and I had shared classrooms, gone around in the same uniform, and suffered under the same demand to succeed. He was a part of my Chilean childhood. What the hell did I care that he had been one of the hunted ones during the dictatorship? I had no idea how, but I wanted to see him, talk to him, help him.

In the entire animal kingdom, keeping firm eye contact between males means a challenge, a test of the will to fight. The policeman's eyes were rocklike. He would not give up. The space between us got denser, more and more tense. We both knew he occupied a far superior position and I had everything to lose and nothing to win. I turned my head and looked toward my gate.

The queue had disappeared. Only the Danish girl and her enormous backpack stood before the two stewardesses behind the counter. She had discovered where I was in the transit hall and waved anxiously at me with her boarding pass. Then she turned to the two stewardesses, and I got the impression she was convincing them not to close up, but to wait for the tardy passenger.

I turned around and looked into the policeman's eyes for the last time. He was a crouching tiger; if he sprang, he would go right for my jugular. There was nothing I could do. I gave up and hurried over to the chair where my carry-on baggage was still lying.

"Did you suddenly decide not to go back to Denmark?" the Danish girl asked me in a humorous voice while I took out my boarding pass. Distracted, I shook my head, and she understood that I did not want to explain my strange behavior.

Inside the plane, we parted, agreeing to talk more later on. How the huge backpack could be accommodated was a mystery to me. She resembled a mutation between a human and a snail staggering in the direction of the pilot's cabin. I went in the opposite direction toward the tail of the plane where I found my seat.

Would Zurita ever know that Palma, his class comrade from Instituto Nacional, searched for him one day in the Santiago airport? Whatever Zurita had done, I hoped with all my heart that the summons over the loudspeakers was just a trivial formality and that later he had been allowed to leave Chile.

I reproached myself for getting so drunk the night before and coming in such poor condition to the airport that I could not react more quickly, and that I had not been more persistent with the policeman in front of the door.

Later, when night overtook the plane, I reproached myself again because perhaps my feelings for Zurita were caused by nothing more than the fear that my adult life in Denmark would make me forget my childhood in Chile. As time passes, I fear more and more the loss of what I had inside me when I came to Denmark. And meeting Zurita and reviving a part of my Chilean past was just a temptation I could not resist. Yes, I reproached myself all the way to France.

On arrival in the Paris airport, I tried to locate the Danish girl, but without success. I had waited far back in the tail of the plane before I could drag myself out. She was probably already on a bus on the way to the gate where the plane to Denmark would take off in an hour.

I arrived at the gate for the flight to Copenhagen and sat down and waited. The stress that comes from powerlessness would not let me relax. I still could not resign myself to the fact that I had been so close to Zurita in Santiago's airport.

Someplace or other near me, Danish was being spoken. Denmark got closer. Where had the Danish girl and her backpack gone? Perhaps she had lost her way in this labyrinth of concrete and plastic.

Suddenly the thought struck me like lightning that Zurita could have been on the same plane to Paris as I was if the loudspeakers had summoned him for some inconsequential reason. Of course! The airport police often take care of certain irregularities that fall outside the area of the airport and airline personal, as, for example, finding the owner of a lost bag or plane ticket. If that were the case, he could have quietly and calmly left the queue I did not want to stand in, gone back to the entrance, arranged there what needed to be arranged, and afterwards returned to the queue and then gotten on the plane. In the meantime I had wandered through my memories and searched for him everywhere else in the transit hall. As far as the policeman's reaction is concerned, well, what was his reaction? There was nothing in his hostile, typically Chilean cop-tone that could provide final proof that Zurita was behind the door he was guarding. Maybe he was not guarding any door at all and was just standing there to keep an eye on the stamping of the passports. Why had I simply assumed Zurita was behind the door?

My own bad experiences in Chilean airports had no doubt muddled my perception of the situation. I happened to remember the year 1974 when I myself had to leave the country in a hurry and saw some of my fellow passengers, refugees like me, detained by the airport police. But since 1990 I had come in and out of Chile without the least problem. So the more I thought about my tense exchange of words with the policeman, the clearer it was I could have misunderstood everything.

And then, too, compared with European airports, Santiago's is a dwarf. I remembered reading the few departure signs at the few gates while I looked for Zurita. Miami, Montevideo, along with a third and maybe a fourth distant, insignificant place. And Paris was undoubtedly the most obvious destination for someone like Zurita.

I reviewed the situation as well as I could, but, when all was said and done, the loudspeakers' paging of Zurita did not unequivocally mean he had been arrested and prevented from leaving the country.

My knowledge of Chilean political conditions was insufficient, but I had heard now and again about a kind of "let's forget" politics where people from both the military and the left who violated the law under the dictatorship, went free because the current government was busy governing and trying to move forward. Zurita could very well have been one of the favored ones.

Suddenly an overwhelming possibility arose that I had sat only a few meters from Zurita, in the same plane, while I was plagued by all sorts of self-reproach. The supposition slowly became a conviction. Zurita had been on the same plane. And the feeling of full-blown absurdity was the only one left to me.

I got up, and in order to shake off this feeling of absurdity, began to walk back and forth. With the same purpose in mind, I tried to divert my attention from my human surroundings, which consisted mainly of Danes and Frenchmen. A group of Frenchmen, looking like business people, stood close to the gate talking together with the obvious intention of also being heard on the other side of the globe. And once more it seemed clear to me that French had an unmasculine, unmusical, and completely ugly sound. Danish, on the other hand, sounded both rhythmic and solid.

How ridiculous that Zurita and I had flown on the same

plane. One's own ridiculousness is obviously easier to bear than the absurdity of life. And suddenly I had the desire to laugh. To what purpose did I reproach myself for a whole night? Did I think, perhaps, that self-flagellation would reconstruct my Chilean past or make me a better, more sensitive, person?

An older Danish woman observed me with a serious demeanor, and I suspected I had laughed aloud or perhaps looked like a schizophrenic.

In Santiago's airport I had imagined Zurita as a hero—a real man and an idealist who had fought and sacrificed himself for his country's freedom. But here in the Paris airport, I saw another Zurita. It was as if my mind had done a somersault and then landed upside down. For the Zurita who had sat in the plane not far from me was a man looking forward to a political meeting or a vacation. And this man was that type of childish and callous psychopath who is fascinated by weapons and explosives. This man was ruthless, indifferent to the loss of a few lives or more, so long as it served his purposes.

In some way or other, I wanted to see Zurita only as a hero. But I could not avoid thinking that I had known a great many individuals of various nationalities with a past history of spying, guerrilla activity, infiltration, military actions and the like. And they have confessed, often with the same words and sentences, that these activities swarm with frustrated psychopaths who do not fight for any cause. They are engaged in "the struggle" for or against something or other because they cannot function at all in normal contexts. In the worst cases you hear about thugs and sadists who switch sides and work for "the enemy" if they get a better offer.

"The ecstatic feeling of being in a film," I have frequently heard in this context. Some of them who used this phrase maintained that when they looked back on their time in "the struggle," they could not recognize themselves at all.

And of course, I remembered the many conversations with Abelardo, a Chilean who, about the same time as Zurita, had taken part in another underground movement against the dictatorship. According to Abelardo, it was quite a task to keep nuts out of the organization. A task that was not always completely successful. The most frequent reason for the members of the organization being caught by the secret police was bragging, stupid childish bragging. There were always some who could not resist letting their girlfriends, family, friends, neighbors, and the whole world know that they were involved in something dangerous and forbidden.

The clock that hung from the ceiling showed that the waiting time had shrunk to ten minutes. Danish daily life waited for me just a few hours from the airport. And strictly speaking, Zurita, hero or psychopath, could go to hell. I sat back and shut my eyes to unwind and, with a little luck, change my train of thought.

And there, in the deep dark interior of my head, I saw Zurita—in a strange and surprising memory. He was about fifteen years old and without his school uniform. I sat in a bus, and it was hot. It must have been during our summer vacation. He walked along Alameda, Santiago's main street, hand in hand with a very beautiful girl, the kind of upper-class girl that was unknown in my neighborhood. He could not know I was observing him from the bus. What a striking difference between his after-school clothes and mine. Everything he was wearing was white: shirt, trousers, and loafers. He instantly reminded me of an incredibly rich German playboy who at the time was visiting Chile with the actress Brigitte Bardot. The French beauty and the stylish German in white clothes were all over the front pages of the newspapers. Zurita was a minicopy of the German—stylish and walking hand in hand with his own beauty. As usual he appeared relaxed. My bus drove farther up Alameda and I lost sight of him. And I said to myself that I had seen Zurita outside of school—and he was just the same as ever.

That I suddenly could remember this minute piece of life I had once lived proved that under the right circumstances the forgotten can be rescued and revived. And it was probably not by chance that I had suddenly remembered that situation. Nor had Zurita's white clothes been fortuitous either, as I had thought that warm summer day on the Alameda.

There could be no other explanation—Zurita had imitated the German from the front pages of the papers. The boy Zurita's charm and notable adult charisma came from his already alienated, cinema-like personality. His chispa to make fun of daily life's high points was solely an expression of the contempt he felt for his surroundings, which years later would make him one of the most wanted terrorists in Chile.

The boy Zurita had grown to a man who no longer found enough pleasure in dismissing others with "Man, I'm in complete agreement with you!" Or by asking the teacher if it was "in the morning or in the afternoon?" Now he would shoot and set off bombs while he acted like a local James Bond. And all to no one's benefit. The military oppression was absolutely not diminished by Zurita's actions—on the contrary. Many innocent people were arrested and mistreated because types like Zurita justified it. And how many policemen from precisely that working class Zurita claimed to defend ended up either wounded or killed because of his actions?

Someone nudged me. It was the Danish girl and her backpack. She didn't say anything but smiled and pointed toward the gate, where people were already boarding. Silently we got on the plane, followed the information on our boarding passes, and again sat a long way from each other.

After the plane took off, food was served, and after the food, fatigue returned. I needed to empty my head of thoughts, to close my eyes and free-fall until sleep got me to rise from reality the same way the plane rose from the earth.

I closed my eyes but could neither keep from thinking nor get to sleep. Zurita the hero and Zurita the psychopath, the two men kept on appearing alternately.

I had to find something, some sign that could bring me closer to Zurita the mystery. But everything I could remember about him had already been remembered. To envision things again, ordinary things from my school days, like school desks, stairs, door handles, windows, and so on, helped me recreate entire situations.

School desks—their surfaces were completely disfigured by our cheating on written tests. A few minutes before a mathematics test, you could read all sorts of formulas on nearly every desk—all of them written with brown pencil and nearly microscopic letters in order to camouflage them in the wooden desk's brown color. Later, during the test, you could calmly consult your desk. After the tests, the writing on the desktop was carefully removed by erasers or scraped off with a razor blade. And then the desk was ready to receive new information. Cheating on tests was a discipline in constant development. You gained esteem by finding daring methods and then venturing to employ them.

It was when I remembered the gate to Instituto Nacional, with its old faithful porter in his cage, that I again came to see Zurita. I was on my way home in the evening. I may have been in sixth or seventh grade. I had just passed the port and found myself next to the main street, Alameda, when a voice behind me called, "Palma." Zurita was walking behind me and gestured that I should wait for him. That surprised me. My class comrades all knew that when I came to Alameda, I always turned to the left in order to take a bus in the direction of the coast and Santiago's middle class and poor neighborhoods. All the others in the class turned to the right in the direction of the Andes Mountains and the upper-class neighborhoods.

"I'm going to the YMCA," he explained.

"Some of the students in our class were members of the

American Christian youth organization, YMCA, whose large building was in the middle of the city near where I took my bus. The YMCA was often mentioned, but I never asked what it was. I did not want to call attention to my considerably lower economic status, which kept me from that kind of after-school interest. Now that there were only the two of us, I thought it might be a good time to ask him about the YMCA. "It's a kind of club," he said, and shrugged his shoulders as if there was nothing more to say. "But, what do you do there?" I asked. Again, he answered casually, "Oh, well...there's a swimming pool, ping-pong, ju-jitsu...lectures and a whole bunch of other things. But I stay in the café where I can sit and talk and fool around with the others. All that other stuff doesn't interest me." At least now I knew a lot more about the YMCA than before.

I hardly ever hung around with my school comrades in my spare time. Why? Again, I could not live up to their require-ments for leisure—fine clothes, eating out, movies, and so on. This walk with Zurita was just as new to me as it was pleasant. We talked and laughed together. Around us darkness was beginning to descend, and colossal Santiago greeted the night by turning on its thousands of lights. We walked through hordes of adults and schoolchildren on their way home from their day's efforts. We passed the usual beggars, shouting newsboys, policemen on their beats, small stands shaped like ships on wheels that sold roasted peanuts, and kiosks covered with magazines and newspapers. Street venders demonstrated the latest thing in spot-removers, children's toys, glasscutters, and so on. And a couple of whores were already posted on their hunting corners. We heard the old motors and vehement horns of the traffic. We saw people fighting with each other to climb into jam-packed buses. And there we walked unconcerned and without haste, protected by the world we created through each other's company. When we passed La Moneda, the government palace, we spoke about what it would be like to have all the power the Chilean president had. In our young eyes it was like owning the country itself with mountains, valleys, rivers, cities and everything. Suddenly Zurita said something about his father meeting the President now and again. That made an impression on me. Zurita's father knew the most powerful man in the country, a kind of Chilean extension of God. A thing like that I would probably already have mentioned at the beginning of our conversation about the President, but for Zurita it was just a minor detail he had remembered casually. When we had to part, he said, "See you tomorrow, Palmita." He smiled, clapped me on the shoulder, and continued down Teatinos Street. Palmita—that meant "little Palma," and it was a warm and friendly way my school comrades sometimes inflected my last name.

The hum of the plane slowly occupied my sense of hearing. A stream of cold air from above hit me in the middle of my face. And a voice on the speakers said something or other incomprehensibly. My eyes still remained closed while I waited for the miracle that would enable me to keep on remembering. But the miracle didn't come. The chain of memories was inexorably broken when Zurita and I parted on Teatinos Street right after passing La Moneda.

Perhaps consciousness can only remain a short moment in the depths of memory—and then it must rise again just as when you are under water and have to come up for air. It must be the self-survival instinct, our only guardian angel, which keeps us from neglecting the present. I opened my eyes, resigning myself to the fact I was unable to force myself to dig up more memories.

Since Santiago's airport, I had remembered Zurita in various situations, but at no time with such intensity as during this walk through the city—because there were just us two, outside the classroom. And I did not have to strain to see his smiling face when he called to me on Alameda. And when he clapped my shoulders in farewell across from La Moneda.

Once more I began to think things through. I had speculated that Zurita, the boy with the special chispa, might have developed into a psychopath who had chosen armed struggle for base reasons. But looking back on the youth of known or even lesser-known assholes, you always find deviant tendencies—the desire to inflict pain on animals and people, a sick need for attention, and self-hatred, tendencies of disloyalty, ass-kissing, and the like. Seven years of school is a long time. And I had never seen any sign of unpleasantness in him.

Zurita was first arrested when he was twenty-nine years old. He began at the university as a boy of seventeen. I faintly remembered that he was one of those talking about becoming a lawyer. And even though he never finished his education, he was intelligent, came from a good family, and had attended what was then Chile's best high school. He was simply destined to have a good life. But he made a choice that meant the renunciation of all advantages most of our school comrades considered to be the very meaning of existence.

Yes, Zurita must have been a true idealist, who completely and totally misjudged the results of an armed struggle against the dictatorship. People ready to die for a cause are undoubtedly more dangerous to their surroundings than to themselves. But in some way or other, I had respect for Zurita.

Maybe it was the usual cheap emotions that appear so easily and can convince me of anything if it just feels right. Remembering my old school comrade's clap on my shoulder and his "Palmita" had really touched me.

But when all was said and done, the newspapers' "terrorist leader" and I had once walked through Santiago after school. And we had been two innocent schoolboys of eleven, united in the belief that only the best awaited us. For that reason I now wished to think the best of him.

My food tray looked like a garbage dump when they took it away. Denmark would soon be in sight and I looked forward to it. My daily life, in spite of its many petty aspects, provides an excellent fixed point in my life. All the doubtful existential matters have to adjust themselves to the concrete tasks of the day—to pay a bill or take the garbage out; and as far as I'm concerned, that is just fine.

The Danish girl came from somewhere in the plane and sat down in the empty seat next to me. We were already beginning to lose altitude. She fastened her seat belt.

"You look pensive," she said.

"I'm just tired," I answered. And that was the nearest I could come to the truth.

"Maybe you're sad," she said.

"Do I look like I am?"

"Maybe you would rather have stayed in Santiago…?"

I shook my head no.

"Wouldn't you rather sit in Gonzalo's café, drinking and talking with him about the good old days in Denmark?"

"No," I said, and added, "I've had enough of remembering."

"What do you mean by that?" she said.

"Just what I said," I answered. "Right now I'm downright tired of remembering."

"Is that possible?"

"You can well believe it."

She seemed satisfied with this brief explanation.

"What can you see?" she asked.

I looked out of the window. "I can see the airport. As I turned toward her, I said, "Beautiful sight."

"Well," she said, and added with comic irony. "I am about to think you are downright happy to return to normality?" She was probably thinking about the contrast to our festive, tourist-like night in Santiago.

"Yes," I said, "I have nothing against my normal life." I know that young people look down on the concept of normality. I asked, "Does that make me a fool?"

She seemed to be thinking. Then she said with an amused, slightly provocative expression, "Maybe."

We looked at each other a moment...and then we laughed. A few seconds later the wheels of the plane hit the Danish asphalt.

An Angel's Kiss

The Angel can't see me. But I can see her. And should her eyes meet mine by chance she won't recognize me, because the first time we met, more than twenty years ago, I meant nothing to her. Nevertheless, she meant so much to me that I'll always be able to recognize her, no matter where or when.

She's standing at the bar, drinking and smoking. Occasionally she bursts into laughter as if she were happy. Maybe she's truly happy. Maybe she's just drunk and boisterous, as I've so often seen her. But however things are, I hope the reason for her laughter is genuine happiness.

The equally drunk man with her looks ravaged too, and his movements are slow and crude like his eyes and everything else about him. I believe he is either a new or potential lover. That's how it seems. They are playing up to one another while each tries to surpass the other in emphasizing the euphoria of the moment. And now I get the feeling that tonight she's lucky…and feels happiness.

The Angel's body sways, indicating a back that has been weakened by the years—another sign that the blows of time strike all the way down to the bone. Her hair is no longer sleek and bright blond—no, not at all. Nor is her skin fresh and healthy, as I'll always remember it.

I know it's stupid to make comparisons, for neither Denmark, she, nor I, nothing can be as it was then. But I can't avoid making comparisons, and while I look at her, I bounce back and forth in time so abruptly that past and present overlap one another. It happens every time I see her.

The man bends forward and sticks his tongue into her obliging mouth. His large hand completely covers one of her breasts the same way you grip a small ball or an orange. This arouses her. She moves back a little and looks at the man with a silence that demands more of him. Then she closes her eyes in order to control herself and becomes one with the rising excitement. And in this deep moment, her face shines, revealing a glimpse of the striking beauty she once possessed.

She was an angel when, suddenly, she stood before me that night at the end of August in 1974, only two days after my arrival in Denmark, and asked me in English if I could give her a cigarette. My English consisted of very few words and sentences, but the word cigarette is easy to understand. Her perfect face, so close to mine, filled me with a confusion I found difficult to conceal.

Even that very first time I saw her in the Copenhagen café, she was so drunk that her body strained to maintain its balance. The sad fact is that I've never seen her sober, never.

While I searched for a cigarette in my jacket pocket, I was surprised to discover that her drunkenness only accentuated the beautiful features of her face. The lower lip drooped a little, revealing even white teeth. The sleepy eyes contained blue seas. The long, golden hair billowed slightly as if caressed by an invisible wind. I guessed she must be about my own age, nineteen or twenty. But the dim light of the café made her resemble the painting of an angel who had only just awakened to the world.

I looked at the three other Chileans with me, and they looked at me. I was not alone in being astonished by this personification of human beauty. The two Chilean women, one of whom I lived with, were just as fascinated as the other guy and me.

I grew up on the outskirts of Santiago in a huge housing project, teeming with incurable alcoholics, but I never saw a single woman drunk. The few and rare cases were found further down at the bottom of the bottom of social misery. And they were viewed as lost creatures, almost as lepers, whom it was better to avoid at any cost. But who would want to avoid this drunken wonder?

I held out my open pack of cigarettes, and she began fumbling in it with shaking fingers. Before she put the cigarette in her mouth, she glanced at my companions. When she turned her eyes toward me again, I held a burning match to the cigarette in her lips. She took a drag and looked at me intently. South Americans were a rare sight in Denmark in 1974. She probably was trying to figure out where I might be from. Then there was a silent, ambiguous moment when I smiled, lost in the sea of her eyes. She smiled, too. Then she took a step forward and kissed me on the cheek…and then stepped back a little and patted me softly on the spot where she had kissed me.

I saw her floating shape move slowly away toward the bar's door. And then she was gone.

One of the Chilean women said, "She was so beautiful," and shook her head. It was clear that at first she had tried to deny the beauty of the Danish girl, but afterwards realized that certain facts are impossible to negate.

My life as a refugee in Denmark had just begun. And after only two days, a drunken angel had kissed me. Could there be any better sign of welcome?

I think it was at least a full three years before I saw her again. At Nørreport Station. I was going down the stairs to take the S-train. And there she stood, talking on one of the pay phones next to the ticket window. The sight of her profile stopped me in my tracks.

I looked back on that night she kissed me. God…it had been an eternity ago—an eternity, which, I knew well enough, had only been three years. I was no longer the new arrival she had kissed. I was twenty-two now and spoke Danish to a Danish common-law wife. And Nørrebro Street was no longer a mystical, dream-like place in a new country, but just a street in Copenhagen, the city where I lived. I had found daily life in Denmark and had become a part of it. And finally, the last three years had given me a few instructive hard blows on my back, without breaking it. Yes, I had become older in body and soul since the night her lips touched my face.

I approached slowly, fearful I might be mistaken and it wasn't her, because then my feelings and reflections would lack a foundation. But I wasn't mistaken. I stopped a few meters from her, pretending I was waiting my turn for the phone. As I expected, she didn't remember me. She glanced at me indifferently and went on smoking and talking into the phone. And she was drunk this time, too.

It was a man she was talking to, a man who meant a great deal to her. I knew that from the mixture of hope and pain that shone in her eyes. And I could hear it in her almost begging voice. She spoke for a long time, and even though she looked at me from time to time, she didn't hurry to finish her conversation. The coins kept on falling into the coin slot, and more of them were waiting on the well-worn telephone book. She had surely prepared herself for this conversation. But the man at the other end of the line didn't have the same feelings for her that she had for him. She still possessed the same dazzling beauty. But she was sad. Tears had begun to run down her cheeks.

I've never been able to understand time. But in rare moments when I'm deepest within myself, I can feel some of time's many faces. At the sight of her I felt both the time that runs with us and the time that runs away from us. Suddenly I stood in the midst of the incomprehensible distance that separated the one she had kissed from the one who observed her as she spoke on the telephone.

And I realized I was now paying the price for the kiss she had given me. I believe what they say is true—everything in life has its price.

On my arrival in Denmark I was liberated from the feeling of before and after. I suddenly found myself in a new world where the course of time was not visible to me. In Denmark there were neither children who had become teenagers nor adults who had become old. Nor were there buildings that had been built up or torn down. In Denmark there were no roads where there hadn't been roads before, nor any places where I'd been as a child or visited a few years or few months ago, either. People and things were as they were. They could not be compared to something they had been previously.

This new world without a past freed me from my own past, and a healing lightness flowed through my body and my actions—for I've always experienced the trail of time as a burden forcing me to surrender to my own past and the crushing feeling of the evanescence of all things.

The Angel hadn't only kissed me; she had also encumbered me with a past in Denmark. And as I watched her speaking on the phone, the tears running down her cheeks, I realized, amazed, that in Denmark, too, time ran inexorably. I would rather have been spared this recognition. I would rather have kept that happy belief I would live forever in a Danish world without any past.

There we stood, only a few meters from each other. And just like Denmark's people and things, I, too, had become an extension of something that had been different before.

I can't reproach her for kissing me without thinking of the consequences. None of us can calculate the results of our actions. Besides, sooner or later something other than her would have forced me to see how the flow of time runs its course everywhere. Even in Denmark.

Suddenly she threw down the receiver. And like that distant evening in 1974, she moved her drunk and swaying figure away from me. Sobbing, she went up the stairs toward the street and the city above until I could no longer see her.

I went over to the telephone, picked up the buzzing receiver, and set it back on its hook. On the telephone book lay the coins that had waited in vain to be used. The Angel who had kissed me welcome to Denmark was sad. The Angel loved without being loved.

159

The third time I saw her, again in Nørrebro, I had lived nearly five years in Denmark. It must have been 1979. I was having a splendid time, drinking heavily with a group of Danes. The bar was to close soon, and we got up from the table to find someplace else where we could enjoy what was left of the night. And there she was.

The surprise sobered me in an instant. She sat facing a man—on a seat just behind my chair, and that's why I hadn't seen her. A number of empty beer bottles and a full ashtray on her table indicated she had probably been at the bar about as long as I had. One of the people with me asked, "Is there something wrong?" And I answered, "No. It's just that I've seen an angel."

I stood there for a few seconds before I had to leave with my companions. And then I discovered it. Wrinkles underlined her eyes, which seemed fatigued and were without sparkle. Her skin had an unhealthy tone. And her hair, which had been pure gold before, now hung faded and lifeless. It was scarcely three years since I'd last seen her at Nørreport. But at least fifteen years had settled over her body.

That night, or rather the rest of that night, I thought of her. I refused to be reconciled to the sight of her vanishing beauty. After a few glasses, I came to the conviction she was an angel in the clutches of some kind of evil power corroding her from the inside.

On the way home, staggering drunkenly through the winter cold and the faded lights of the night, I imagined crazy things—that she appeared out of the street's shadows and I had the courage and strength to prevent her perdition, to fight and save her, just as heroes from bygone ages had done for beautiful women. I would tell her how much her kiss meant to me when I first arrived. And I would kiss her and pat her on the cheek, as she had done for me, until she was healthy and beautiful again. Yes…that winter night I was ready to become a hero for her sake.

After that night, my years in Denmark kept flowing by, furtive, almost unnoticed, and with the sole purpose of never returning again. And it happened that I saw her here and there, each time where I least expected it.

They order more beer. And while the bartender goes about filling their order, he looks at them out of the corner of his eye and smiles knowingly to himself. He certainly remembers the many couples who had found each other on the other side of his bar.

She's not having much luck with men is the feeling I have—most likely because I've always seen her alone and drunk or in the company of different men. Never with the same man. I also imagine that the extraordinary beauty she once had prevented her somehow from finding happiness with one man. Perhaps, like other beautiful women, she's had too easy a time with men and unconsciously sought the unattainable, and its pain. I don't know. It's just a feeling I have, nothing more.

I've never spoken to her. That's something I know, but it suddenly occurs to me now, as if it were something new. Our only contact was the cigarette she asked me for in 1974, and I gave it to her without saying a word. From that moment, silence and distance seem to have settled between us for good.

For the first time, I wish she were alone. I could not care less about the man, but of course I have to consider that he could feel provoked if I just go over now and talk with her. Another thing is…I don't think the man can possibly imagine how beautiful the woman in front of him once was. And even less will he be able to imagine how much she meant to me and why.

But I can't avoid thinking: what will I get out of speaking with her? Because I really don't know. Anyway, I really wish I could go over to her freely and say something like "Many, many years ago you kissed me. Your kiss made me feel welcome in Denmark. It filled me with optimism and the belief that I found myself in a good country. And who knows? My life might have been entirely different if you hadn't kissed me. I want you to know how much I believe in the significance of certain small, apparently unimportant things..."

There is so much she doesn't know. She can hardly imagine that my past in Denmark began with her. It's even less likely she knows that there was once a time she made me behave so foolishly that afterwards I felt ashamed.

It happened one sunny afternoon not too long ago. I cycled up Nørrebro Street on the way to my apartment. I was off in the endless daydreaming that overtakes cyclists when I sensed something or other near me. It was a young girl cycling beside me who was observing me with greater interest than the situation called for. And when she saw that I had noticed it, she smiled at me. It's one of Denmark's brighter sides that girls smile so easily. I smiled back. We turned our eyes away from each other and went on cycling. At the next traffic light we stopped and exchanged a few friendly glances. Under the sun, her smile seemed to shine even brighter, and as I asked myself why, she said, "I don't think you know it, but I've seen you many times before."

"Have you?" I asked, surprised.

"It was many years ago that I saw you for the first time," she said, and began to cycle again.

I began to cycle, too, all the while thinking that I couldn't place her face in any context and that she was fifteen or twenty years younger than my forty years. And yet she had seen me for the first time many years ago.

An irresistible curiosity took hold of every nerve in my body. What had I done to get a place in this young girl's memory? I asked her, "Would you like to have a cup of coffee?" And it sounded absolutely stupid, as if I had a thermos of fresh coffee in one hand and a cup in the other. Of course, I meant a cup of coffee at a café.

For a quick moment she looked down at her bicycle's

front wheel, with a tinge of helplessness, and without looking up at me, shook her head.

What an enigmatic way of saying no—as if because of some powerful command, she must not have anything at all to do with me. And it was clear that I should not insist. But I lost my head. Nearly against my will, because I already knew the answer, I said:

"Let's have a cup of coffee together."

Again she shook her head without looking at me.

"Why not?" I asked, already feeling embarrassed.

She kept on looking at some distant spot far from the bicycle path. She just shut me out.

"But, why not?" I asked again.

This time she looked at me with an empty, hopeless expression that didn't belong to so young a face. I could ask for the next hundred years, and she still wouldn't accept.

I no longer felt embarrassed. Now I felt ashamed, so I wouldn't ask again.

We stopped at the next traffic light and turned our faces toward each other. I realized she saw something in me she had seen before. And as far as I was concerned, there was nothing else to do except find myself in the knowledge she had of me.

We began cycling again. Then she said, "I have to turn here," and pointed at the next street corner.

"Be well," I said when we came to the corner.

Suddenly it seemed as if she wanted to say something, reveal what she owed me. I waited. But then she said, "Thanks, and you, too." Then she turned. And I've never seen her again.

The following days I kept picturing the girl on the bicycle and her enigmatic face. Perhaps she had met me at some quite special moment in time, when she was either very happy or very sad. Perhaps she had dropped something, which out of mechanical friendliness I had picked up for her. Perhaps she simply had a good memory and could remember me when I passed her in the street many years ago. Perhaps I knew her parents and had seen her as a child. Something or other enabled her to remember me.

But more important than where she knew me from was— Why had I behaved so foolishly? Why did I keep on insisting on that idiotic cup of coffee? Why was I almost desperate to talk with her?

I sought the answer in every single word she had said, in every single movement she had made. We had shared a rare mood, which shut out Copenhagen, the summer weather, and the unpredictable streets—a mood that included just the two of us. And then I got it. She had looked at me and at herself in all the situations where she had seen me before. I had reminded her of what she had been. I had shown her what she had become. She had seen the inexorable flow of time. And her helpless look was due to her belief that I would never understand all the things she saw when she looked at me. Her youth didn't allow her to understand that I, too, was familiar with the experience my presence gave her. It was the very same experience the Angel gave me.

The girl on the bicycle and I had something in common. But, like her, I'd not known what it was. Now I understood the urge to know more about her, to hear her talk—and why I'd behaved like a fool.

I'm certain that if I plumb and scrutinize the depths of my mind, I'll find other similar situations where the Angel has influenced me to choose one course of action or another. But no, I've no desire to set out on such an expedition into my own interior. For the most part, it's just fine not knowing why one does one thing and not another.

Now something's happening. What's happening is the man is sticking his hand under her skirt between her thighs, probably to touch her between the legs. Then he bends over and whispers something in her ear, which makes her laugh and rub her cheek against his. Pleasure always seeks eternity. And she presses her cheek hard against his and looks up at the ceiling, toward the night sky and the stars, which she cannot see. He pulls away abruptly and walks toward the toilets. And suddenly she's standing alone at the bar.

I get up and hesitate a moment. It isn't easy to break a silence and distance that has survived for more than twenty years. But if I don't do it now, then when? I go over and stand in the spot where the man was standing before. And since I still don't know what I'll do or say, I pretend to be waiting to order something from the bartender. On the other side of the bar, I can see her and myself in the mirror. And there I see the irritation with which she observes me. An outsider has stolen her man's place. An invader has trod on the happiness she has built up over the evening.

I turn and look at the tired light in her eyes. I look at the skin hiding behind a layer of make-up, and at those lips, which kissed me when I was young and Denmark an eternal, timeless place. And I could say to her, "There was once a winter night where I would have fought anyone for you. Do you know that for years I've called you Angel? And do you know that when I see you, I see many things—mostly time, but also how utterly small and insignificant we humans are when all is said and done." I could also say quite simply what the girl on the bicycle said to me—"I don't think you know it...but I've seen you many times before."

"What are you staring at?"

She has spoken to me. And this voice is not an angel's voice. But where are angels found if not in the longing and dreams of people?

"Tell me...is there something wrong with you, or what?"

I have to say or do something. Suddenly I know what.

"Do you have a cigarette?" I ask, realizing I'm speaking to her as I would to a person I've known for a long time. A cigarette...I'd given up smoking some years ago.

Annoyed, she sighs and looks into her cigarette pack while her tightened lips suggest a kind of calculation.

"No, I don't have too goddamned many," she says. And she adds dismissively, "Can't help you."

It was one of the answers I had expected. "That's all right," I say, trying to smile. "Thank you, anyway."

I beat a retreat from her eyes, which want me gone, long gone from her and the happiness she awaits this evening.

Outside the bar, the city seems so still, as if it isn't breathing at all. I listen…it seems to me the city lives, nourishing itself with a single, infinite breath. How strange! Copenhagen can still surprise me.

It's probably best I go home—for I know that small, apparently insignificant things can in reality mean a great deal. And so, when I get home, I'll look out of my window toward Nørrebro Street…and I'll think about why the Angel wouldn't give me the cigarette that more than twenty years ago I gave to her.

Born in Santiago, Chile in 1954, Rubén Palma grew up in one of Santiago's working class quarters where poverty and criminality were part of everyday life. Fortunately, and thanks to his mother's dedication, he finished high school in 1971. He left the University of Chile after only three months to pursue his own studies in esoteric and eastern philosophies. During this period he made a living selling antiquarian books at a flea market. Later he participated actively in what he believed was a libertarian, leftist movement but later became disenchanted with its authoritarian nature. These turbulent, youthful activities and a desertion from the army in 1973, right after the military coup in Chile, forced him to leave the country. In 1974, at the age of 19, aided by the World Council of Churches, he managed to get travel documents and escape to Buenos Aires, Argentina, where he became a refugee under the protection of the United Nations. The unstable political situation made Argentina a dangerous place for refugees but, thanks to the kind help of the Danish consul in that country, he was relocated in Denmark in August 1974. In his first years in Denmark, he worked at various jobs, such as dishwasher, translator, and dockworker. Since 1985, he has been employed by the Danish Red Cross. Denmark became his new home and new country, so much so that after 25 years in Denmark he was writing in Danish and receiving high praise from Danish reviewers for his creative work. Author of three works of fiction, Mr. Palma has also written children's stories and plays. He currently lives in Copenhagen.

Danish critics recognized his talent immediately and praised his solid creation of characters, his dramatic skills in plotting, and his range of tone. As Michael Zangenberg perceptively notes in his review in *Politiken*, "Salman Rushdie coined the phrase 'the countries of the fantasy' to describe those strange places between a country forever lost and a new one, one that will never be familiar or felt as one's own. Rubén Palma sends ten bittersweet, mainly autobiographical, postcards from this borderland. But he also expands the field to embrace the gap between the two sexes, between two national languages and cultures, between life and death, between past and future."

A Note on the Translation

The translator has striven to be faithful to the sense and tone of the Danish text; however, a few minor changes, omissions, and additions have been made (with the agreement of the author) with the U.S. audience in mind, and in order to achieve greater clarity and provide cultural background where necessary.

CURBSTONE PRESS, INC.

is a nonprofit publishing house dedicated to literature that reflects a commitment to social change, with an emphasis on contemporary writing from Latino, Latin American and Vietnamese cultures. Curbstone presents writers who give voice to the unheard in a language that goes beyond denunciation to celebrate, honor and teach. Curbstone builds bridges between its writers and the public – from inner-city to rural areas, colleges to community centers, children to adults. Curbstone seeks out the highest aesthetic expression of the dedication to human rights and intercultural understanding: poetry, testimonies, novels, stories, and children's books.

This mission requires more than just producing books. It requires ensuring that as many people as possible learn about these books and read them. To achieve this, a large portion of Curbstone's schedule is dedicated to arranging tours and programs for its authors, working with public school and university teachers to enrich curricula, reaching out to underserved audiences by donating books and conducting readings and community programs, and promoting discussion in the media. It is only through these combined efforts that literature can truly make a difference.

Curbstone Press, like all nonprofit presses, depends on the support of individuals, foundations, and government agencies to bring you, the reader, works of literary merit and social significance which might not find a place in profit-driven publishing channels, and to bring the authors and their books into communities across the country. Our sincere thanks to the many individuals, foundations, and government agencies who have supported this endeavor: Connecticut Commission on the Arts, Connecticut Humanities Council, Eastern CT Community Foundation, Fisher Foundation, Greater Hartford Arts Council, Hartford Courant Foundation, J. M. Kaplan Fund, Lamb Family Foundation, Lannan Foundation, John D. and Catherine T. MacArthur Foundation, National Endowment for the Arts, Open Society Institute, Puffin Foundation, United Way, and the Woodrow Wilson National Fellowship Foundation.

Please help to support Curbstone's efforts to present the diverse voices and views that make our culture richer. Tax-deductible donations can be made by check or credit card to:
Curbstone Press, 321 Jackson Street, Willimantic, CT 06226
phone: (860) 423-5110   fax: (860) 423-9242
www.curbstone.org

IF YOU WOULD LIKE TO BE A MAJOR SPONSOR OF A CURBSTONE BOOK, PLEASE CONTACT US.